Mia Couto was born in Beira, Mozambique, in 1955. During the years after the independence of his country in 1975, he was the director of the Mozambique Information Agency, and editor of the magazine *Tempo* and the Maputo newspaper *Notícias*. He lives in Mozambique and works as an environmental biologist.

His first collection of poetry, *Raiz de Orvalho (Root of Dew)* was published in 1983. In 1986, his first book of short stories, *Vozes Anoitecidas*, received wide critical acclaim in Portugal. Since then, he has published four further collections of short stories and two novels, *Terra Sonâmbula* (1992) and *A Varanda do Frangipani* (1996), published by Serpent's Tail in 2001 as *Under the Frangipani*. His work has been translated into several European languages, and some of his stories have been adapted for the stage in Mozambique and South Africa.

Also by Mia Couto and published by Serpent's Tail
Under the Frangipani

A police inspector is investigating a strange murder, a case in which all the suspects are eager to claim responsibility for the act.

Set in a former Portuguese fort which stored slaves and ivory, *Under the Frangipani* combines fable and allegory, dreams and myths with an earthy humour. The dead meet the living, language is invented, reality is constantly changing.

In a story which is partly a thriller, partly an exploration of language itself, Mia Couto surprises and delights, and shows just why he is one of the most important African writers of today.

'Mia Couto is a white man with an African soul' Henning Mankell

'This is an original and fresh tale quite unlike anything else I have read from Africa. I enjoyed it very much' Doris Lessing

'Couto's tale unfolds on two levels: first, as a mystery story, for the fantastic confessions generate a "whodunit" suspense; more demandingly as a thematic puzzle' *TLS*

'To read Mia Couto is to encounter a peculiarly African sensibility, a writer of fluid, fragmentary narratives...a remarkable novel' *New Statesman*

'Blending history, death and a uniquely African flavour of magic realism, *Under the Frangipani* is a powerful and trenchant evocation of life in a society traumatised by decades of war and poverty' *New Internationalist*

'Anything but an everyday whodunit...it is a novel which forces the reader to question preconceived notions, to take a second look at assumptions that normally go unnoticed and to try to look at the world with fresh, unspoiled eyes' *Worldview*

The Last Flight of the Flamingo

Mia Couto

Translated by David Brookshaw

Library of Congress Catalog Card Number: 2003111417

A complete catalogue record for this book can be obtained from the British Library on request

First published as *O último voo do flamingo* by Editorial Caminho, S.A., Lisboa in 2000

First published in 2004 by Serpent's Tail,
4 Blackstock Mews, London   N4 2BT
website: www.serpentstail.com

Typeset at Neuadd Bwll, Llanwrtyd Wells
Printed and bound by CPI Group (UK) Ltd, Croydon, CR0 4YY
10   9   8   7   6   5   4   3   2

Translation funded by the Arts Council of England

To Joana Tembe and João Joãoquinho,
who told me stories as if praying

Contents

It was I who transcribed the talk that follows into visible Portuguese. Nowadays, they are voices I no longer listen to except from within my blood, as if their recollection came to me not from memory but from the depths of my body. That's the price I pay for having been present at such events. At the time they occurred, I was a translator working for the administration at Tizangara. I witnessed everything narrated here, I heard confessions, I read statements. I put down everything on paper as my conscience demanded. I was accused of lying, falsifying evidence of murder. I was charged. I cannot accept that I lied. But what happened can only be told in words that are as yet unborn. Now, I shall tell you everything in accordance with my one and only wish. Which is a need to free myself of these memories, just as a murderer frees himself of his victim's body.

We were in the first few years after the end of the war and all seemed to be going well, contrary to the general expectation that acts of violence would never cease. The United Nations soldiers had already arrived to supervise the peace process. They came, demonstrating the same insolence as any military force. Poor souls, they believed they were the masters of frontiers, able to manufacture concord.

It all began with them, the blue helmets. They exploded. Yes, that's what happened to those soldiers. They quite simply started to explode. One today. Another one tomorrow. Until, in all, five of them had died.

Now, let me ask you this: did they really and truly explode? That's what they call it for lack of a verb. For an exploded man will always leave some residue of his substance. But in this case, there was nothing left at all. Between being done up and being undone, nothing remained of their original format. Did the soldiers of peace die? Were they killed? I'll leave you to seek the answer in the following pages.

(Signed: the translator of Tizangara)

Loved ones make themselves remembered through tears.
Forgotten ones make themselves remembered through blood.

(A saying from Tizangara)

1 A large sexual organ on the loose

The world is not what exists, but what happens.
(A saying from Tizangara)

To put it crudely and rudely, here's what happened: a severed penis was found right there on the trunk road just outside Tizangara. A large organ on the loose. The locals stood thunderstruck at their discovery. Folk turned up from all around. A ring of people thickened around the object. I was there too, at the rear end of the crowd, standing more in than out. Here's my advice: behind is where you get the best view and you're less visible. The saying is true: if a pin falls into a well, many people watch, but few go down to fetch it.

In our town, events were things that never happened. In Tizangara, the only facts are supernatural ones. And against these facts, everything is an argument. That's why everyone rushed there but no one pulled back. And it took up a whole day, a ring of curious onlookers, cooking up rumours. Doubts were voxpopulated to all and sundry, orders spontaneified in the blinking of an eye.

—*Someone pick that thing up before it gets run over.*

—*Run over or run into?*

—*Poor fellow, he was crippled in his middle!*

The crowd rustled and bustled as if at the market. Then, amidst the general air of puzzlement, someone suddenly glimpsed a blue cap hanging in the sky.

—*Look up there, on top of the tree!*

It was one of those caps worn by the soldiers of the United Nations. Hanging from a branch, it swayed at the whim of the breeze. The moment the identity of the cap was confirmed, it was like a knife thrust through the general murmuring. Straightaway, the crowd washed their hands of it. It was no use twiddling one's thumbs in the confusion. And people dispersed quickly, remarking on how nothing had happened, and even expressing surprise at what they had never seen. And they changed the topic of the conversation:

—*Rain's coming and the wind will get wet.*

—*Yes, we'd better get back to our business.*

—*Let's get out of here, lads!*

And they broke up all in a muddle, leaving the orphaned attachment behind on the hot asphalt. Up on the wizened branch, the missionary hat remained, all alone in the breeze. Blue on a background of blue.

I lingered there all alone, with a strange feeling of foreboding. A thorn was hurting me deep down in my soul. Or to put it another way, I was sucking the sourness out of vinegar. It wasn't yet the event itself, but preparations for its arrival. When silence casts its light around us, that's when we listen to our darkest premonitions. It was then that I was surprised by a gruff voice:

—*You're wanted!*

—*Wanted? Me?*

I knew only too well who the messenger was: it was Chupanga, the administrator's adjutant. An unctuous, servile man – a boot-licker. Like all pleasers, he was submissive towards the mighty and arrogant towards the lowly. The fellow pretended he didn't know me, busy in his appearance of superiority. I even made to shake his hand, but he started to feign shortness of time. A donkey in the company of a lion no longer passes the time of day with a horse.

—*Aren't you the one who speaks other languages affluently?*

—*I speak a couple of languages, yes.*

—*Local or international ones?*

—*Both. Some of them for the road, others for cutting through the undergrowth.*

The messenger clicked his heels like a soldier. That sound, concise as it was, seemed like a warning to me. It was like an angel sneaking through the suburbs of the air. And indeed it was. The angels see what is not happening. At that precise moment, the first problems were beginning, street corners from where my destiny would be led into labyrinths. Somewhere outside me, Chupanga was insisting:

—*You're wanted by His Excellency.*

His Excellency was the administrator. An order from him was not to be doubted. We listen, keep quiet and silently pretend to obey. It's not even worth displaying defiance. Was there ever a soul whose teeth appeared before his lips? The smaller a place, the greater the extent of our obedience.

So that was how, some moments later, I marched, erect and direct, into the headquarters of the administration. It was the same building as in colonial times, but purged of bad spirits. The big old house had been treated by the witchdoctor, in accordance with old beliefs. The voice of command was quick and tuneful in tone:

—*Come in, my friend. We need your services.*

Estêvão Jonas, the town administrator, filled the entire doorframe. His face dripped concern. A white handkerchief swished to and fro, wiping his brow. A generator filled the place with noise and the administrator had to raise his voice:

—*Come in, my comrade ... I mean, my friend.*

I went in. Inside, it was cooler. On the ceiling, a fan spread the air around. Like everyone else in town, I knew the administrator Jonas had diverted the hospital generator for his own private uses. Dona Ermelinda, his wife, had emptied the infirmaries of equipment destined for the general public: fridges, a stove, beds. It had even come out in a newspaper in the capital as a story about the abuse of power. Jonas laughed: he didn't abuse anyone; the others just didn't have any power whatsoever. And he repeated the saying: a goat eats wherever it's tethered.

—*I sent for you because we need some immediate action.*

The administrator even managed to make his voice frown. With good reason and motive: an official delegation was on its way. It was coming to investigate the case of the severed sexual organ. There would be people from the internal government as well as representatives of the external one. There would even be people from the United Nations. They were all coming to investigate the case of the chopped organ. And the other cases involving blue helmets who had disappeared. The town of Tizangara had never received such important figures before. Estêvão Jonas's voice trembled as he pointed at me and said:

—*So you have been appointed official translator with immediate effect.*

—*Translator? But into what language?*

—*That doesn't matter. Any government worthy of respect has its translators. You are to be my personal translator. Do you understand?*

I didn't understand, but I had learned that in Tizangara nothing needed to be understood. I got as far as clearing my throat to suggest my objections. But at that moment Dona Ermelinda, the administrator's wife, arrived. She had made herself known as 'The First Lady'. She looked at me as if I didn't even warrant the status of a human being. And she spoke as if doing the world a great favour.

—*They say there's an Italian coming and that he's going to stay here to conduct the investigation. Do you speak Italian?*

—*No, I don't.*

—*Excellent, because Italians never speak Italian.*

—*But begging your pardon, sir, what language should I translate into?*

—*English, German. One of those, it doesn't matter. We'll get by.*

The administrator's lady wife cut in again, poaching her husband's visibility. As she spoke, she rearranged her turban and shook her long gown. Ermelinda claimed that this was a typically African dress. But we were Africans in both flesh and soul, and we had never seen such a costume. At that point, she repeated:

—*What I want, speaking from my own point of view as Ermelinda, is for them to realise that here in Tizangara, we have simultaneous translation.*

She fiddled with her fingers, tidying their ornaments. She exhibited more rings than Saturn. Turning to her husband, she asked whether culture had been summoned.

—*Culture?*

—*Yes, the dance groups.*

—*They refuse to come. Without payment, they won't agree to anything.*

—*But doesn't anyone do anything out of love in this place anymore?*

The First Lady wanted to know whether there was still a crowd of people on the road. For she wanted to make an official visit to the place where the incident had occurred. Her husband asked awkwardly:

—*Are you going to take a look at the thing, Ermelinda?*

—*Yes, I am.*

—*Do you know what it is, all dead and wizened in the middle of the road?*

—*Yes, I do.*

—*I don't think it's a good idea that a woman of your status … with all those people watching.*

—*I'm going, but not as Ermelinda. I shall go there*

officially, in my capacity as First Lady. And in the meantime, clear the place of all that rabble.

    —*But how can I have the masses dispersed?*

    —*Haven't I told you to buy some sirens? Down south, in the nation, don't the chiefs go round with a siren?*

And off she went in queenly fashion. In the doorway, she shook her tresses, causing her bits of gold to twinkle, multiplied in showy necklaces over her vast bosom.

2   The mission of inquiry

That which is not allowed to flower at the right moment ends up exploding later.
(Another saying from Tizangara)

The town was seething like an ants' nest. Word had been going around that a very important delegation with Mozambican and United Nations soldiers was about to arrive. There was also a top brass from the international force coming too. Along with the foreign soldiers, there would be a non-governmental minister and one or two heads of various departments. And along with them, a certain Italian by the name of Massimo Risi, of no known rank. This was the person who would be stopping for a while at Tizangara.

I was already in the square, lined up along with the heads of the local administration. We were the reception committee and would be responsible for representing our town's good name. The administrator, Estêvão Jonas, was in an anxious twist. He was issuing orders and then unissuing them, and for every time he made us line up, he unlined us thirty times.

—*Get in line!*— he kept shouting, as he surveyed our positions.

But even though he was at his wits' end, he still showed off, his chest rounder than a pigeon after a mate. And so, all dandified, his skin glowed even darker, his brow beaded with glittery drops.

The crowd displayed a prominent banner with huge letters on it: '*Welcome to our Soviet comrades! Long live the internationalism of the proletariat!*' The administrator immediately ordered the banner to be withdrawn. And there'd be no long living to anyone. The people were somewhat confused with regard to the current times.

—*Distribute our own banners, the ones we had painted yesterday.*

—*It would be better if we didn't, Your Excellency.*

—*And why not?*

—*It's because the paint has disappeared from the warehouse.*

—*And what about the cloth?*

—*The cloth didn't disappear. That was stolen.*

They were discussing these discordances when a dappled goat appeared in front of us. The animal was out of tune with the gravity of the occasion. The administrator hissed in a low voice:

—*Who's this goat?*

—*Whose*— his secretary corrected him discreetly.

—*Yes, whose is that piece of shit?*

—*Isn't the goat one of yours, Excellency?*

The order to evacuate the caprine creature came too late: the square was suddenly overflowing with the sound of sirens. In an instant, the speedy vehicles filled the square with dust and noise. Then suddenly, there was a screech of brakes. And a dull thud could be heard, the crash of a car knocking into a body. It was the goat. The creature flew higher than a feathery snipe and fell clattering on to a nearby pavement. It didn't die straightaway. For the time being, it lay there, spattered and battered, bellowing ever more loudly against the world. As a result of the collision, one of the goat's horns flew off with such force that it skimmed off Chupanga, the adjutant. The man picked up the orphaned horn and passed it to the administrator.

—*This is yours, Excellency.*

Estêvão Jonas angrily hurled the horn to the ground. Tugging furiously at my sleeve, he uttered a curt order in undertones:

—*Go and kill that son-of-a-bitch of a goat for me.*

There was no way I could carry out the order. The visitors were already pompously alighting from their cars and the administrator, in anguish, repeated his meaningless command:

—*Get in line!*

Thinking that the order was being issued to them, the people lined up almost in single file. The square was turned into something resembling a parade ground. Estêvão Jonas busied himself with the introductions. But his voice was continually stifled by the bleating of the goat.

—*Here we have ...*

—*Baaah!*

Ideological sabotage was how the administrator later classified such sonorous interruptions. Who else would want to disrupt the splendour of such a solemn occasion? In the circumstances, however, the moment had to be overcome, they had to dust themselves down and keep going. The minister took charge of the situation and issued his instruction:

—*Let's go to the scene of the occurrence.*

It was difficult to find an inch of space. The townspeople thronged together, amazed to witness so many eminent figures parading. All of them brought there because of a male sexual organ, and a recumbent one at that? And the good folk of Tizangara clustered together. Some of them were surprised to see me there, among the worthy. Was I now eating from the pot of the powerful, benefiting from their stove? Others waved to me with improvised respect, just in case I was in a position to do any favours.

The recent arrivals were losing their security cover as they forced their way through the crowds to the place of the grisly discovery. There, among the rabble, one couldn't make out which dignitary was which. Dona Ermelinda, next to her spouse, mumbled to him:

—*Did you hear the sirens? Couldn't you ask them to let us have them when they leave?*

The foreigners anxiously clutched their cameras against their bellies, in case the devil managed to spirit them away. In the midst of the uproar, amongst all the pushing and shoving, the administrator could still be heard issuing his order:

—*Get in line!*

Finally, they got to the high road, where the anonymous organ lay. They formed a circle round it, knotted in silence. Speechless, it was as if they were quietly paying their respects. The fact that the said attachment had lasted all that time without having been removed by animals invited all to exercise their fancy.

Eventually, the representative of central government, after much jangling of his empty pockets, coughed and pondered a metaphysical question: was that thing in the middle of the road an organ or an organism? If it was an organ, disparate and desperate as it was, from whom had it been cut? The subject was enough to spark an unfocussed debate. Clearly, this dusting of voices was designed to scare off the silence. Finally, the local administrator suggested:

—*With all due respect, Your Excellencies: suppose we summon Anna Godwilling?!*

—*And who is this Anna?*— the minister asked.

There was a crisscrossing of voices: how could anyone not know the Godwilling woman? She, the town's whore, the most knowledgeable expert in local manhood.

—*Whores? Have you even got them here?*

And the administrator, puffed with pride, murmured:

—*It's all because of decentralisation, Minister, we are encouraging local initiative!*— And he repeated, swollen with pride: —*Our own Anna!*

The minister thought it best to nip his growing enthusiasm in the bud:

—*Our own, that is ...*

But the administrator was going at full throttle. And he

.pressed on: this Anna was a woman of a thousand imperfections, an artist of invariable routines, a woman whose bonnet was easy to open. She alone would be able to offer a definite opinion on the identity of such an organ. Or was she not an expert in illegal medicine?

—*Do you see, Your Excellency? We'll summon Anna Godwilling to identify the relevant part.*

—*Relevant part?*

—*Part … I mean the thing. The matter pending, so to speak.*

And thereupon, he began to give orders, with military precision, just in case the foreigners began to think the hammer had no handle:

—*Adjutant, go and call Anna Godwilling.*

The messenger was setting off at the double, when he stopped and turned in his tracks and, within public earshot, asked the administrator:

—*I'm sorry, Your Excellency, but where may I find the said lady?*

Estêvão Jonas cleared his throat awkwardly. Now how in heaven's name should he know where to find the creature? And calling the adjutant over to him, he muttered:

—*You idiot! Don't tell me you don't know where to go!*

It was no more than a fraction of a second and the order was carried out. In the meantime, the administrator turned to me and ordered:

—*Translate, translate for Mr Risi!*

—*There's no need, he's followed everything.*

—*Well, sum things up for him at least. Take the opportunity to introduce him to … I mean, explain who our Godwilling woman is.*

There was no time. Anna Godwilling was already making her appearance, without the siren that had heralded the delegation's arrival, but with more of an entrance. The woman exhibited too much flesh and not enough dress. Her high heels sank into the sand like the eyes that skewered her curves. The townsfolk round about gazed at her as if she were not real. Until recently, there hadn't been a prostitute in the town. There wasn't even a word for such a creature in the local language. Anna Godwilling was always an occasion for rapture and desire.

The woman excused herself when she realised the official nature of her summons. Chupanga, as greasy as butter, murmured a brief explanation of the circumstances in her ear. So she hadn't been summoned for her usual services. Anna received the surprising news, all of a posture. Then she let her charms slip, and her voice took on a serious tone. So she had come there, sails billowing, for no reason at all. What was the point of her art if there was no artifice? The woman stroked her false hair and sighed:

—*What a pity! I thought I'd been called out on a job. And with extras for express service.*

She let out a provocative laugh. Then she walked over to the administrator's wife and gazed at her defiantly. She was measuring her height dismissively. When it came to it, who was more of a first lady? With her chin raised, and half smiling, she asked:

—*And how is our First Lady?*

Dona Ermelinda had eyes that spat. Her husband shepherded her away, avoiding disorder.

—*Go home, woman.*

—*It would be better if she stayed*— the prostitute corrected him —*and if we went together to see the remains of the accident. Who knows, she might be able to identify the object?*

The confrontation stopped at that point. For the uniformed foreigners circled the prostitute, sniffing her intense aromas. The members of the delegation began to show their interest: was it that they were zealous, or just curious? And they asked her for proof of her mileage: her curriculum vitae, her participation in sustainable development projects, her work within the community.

—*Do you doubt me? I'm a lawful whore. I'm not one of those jamless tarts. I've even slept with …*

—*Enough, enough*— the minister hastened, and he immediately began to discourse about vague matters, such as whether rain was predicted, the disgraceful state of the roads and other nonsense.

Anna Godwilling answered all his questions by word and gesture, while looking all the while at the Italian. After the quizzing, she went over to Massimo Risi and whispered in his ear. No one heard what it was she said. All folk could see was the white man turn red and then pale again, all bashful and hangdog.

Then the prostitute turned her back on the delegation and went over to the polemical discovery lying on the road. She looked at the disfigured organ, fallen like some flaccid worm. She knelt down and, with a little stick, turned the fleshy hyphen over. A circle formed round Anna Godwilling in anxious anticipation. Silence fell. Until the police chief asked:

—*Was that thing cut off the man or was it vice versa?*

—*That thing, as you call it, doesn't belong to any man from around here.*

—*Are you sure?*

—*Without a shadow of a doubt.*

When she had completed her examination, Anna Godwilling shook her hands and agitated her straightened hair as if she were royalty. The minister called the United Nations representative aside. They conferred:

—*I'm sorry to have to say this, but I think it's another of those cases ...*

—*What cases?*— the foreigner asked.

—*Those cases of explosions.*

—*Surely not!*

—*I'm telling you, it's another explosion.*

—*Don't come to me with that nonsense about explosions. I'm sorry, but I don't buy that one.*

—*But as a minister, I get information ...*

—*Now listen: five soldiers have already vanished. Five! I've got to write a report for my bosses in New York, and I don't want hearsay or stories.*

—*But my government ...*

—*Your government is receiving a lot. Now it's time for you to give something in exchange. And what we want is a plausible explanation!*

And the representative of the world imposed his conditions: he demanded a bilingual report, a forecast of spending requirements and presentation of accounts forthwith. The head of the mission was foaming with rage:

—*Things have just gone too far: five, and now with this one, six!*

Six United Nations soldiers had been eclipsed, leaving no trace except for a river of delirious rumours. How could foreign soldiers disappear into thin air like that, dissolved into dust in the middle of Africa, which is tantamount to saying, in the middle of nowhere? The minister, offended, replied:

—*Very well, I'll go and talk to the wh... to the prostitute.*

—*That's right, talk. What I want is for light to be shed on the subject. And listen: I want everything on tape. I don't want tittle-tattle, I'm tired of folk tales.*

—*But the statements all agree: the soldiers explode!*

—*Explode? How can they explode without landmines, or grenades, or explosives? Don't come to me with chatter. I want everything on tape, right here.*

He handed him a tape recorder and a box of cassettes. A solemn silence ensued. So as to disguise his apparent humiliation, the minister twiddled the knobs on the machine. Suddenly, there was a burst of music from the recorder, warm sounds were released into the air and the people instinctively began to dance. In an instant, the universe had turned into an endless dance floor. In his confusion, the minister got his fingers mixed up, and couldn't stop the racket straightaway. Eventually the music fell silent but some couples still went on twirling. Further away, the goat bleated ever more faintly.

—*What's that?*— asked one of the dignitaries.

—*It's nothing, just children imitating ... I mean playing*—the administrator declared hurriedly.

The United Nations official was like a dragon, blowing flames through his nostrils. He looked up at the heavens as if begging for some divine understanding. He called Massimo Risi and gave him quick final instructions. Then, he got into his spacious vehicle, slamming the door angrily. But the jeep wouldn't start: was the driver nervous or the battery flat? The engine groaned at every failed attempt. The representative of the world, from behind closed windows, was no doubt waiting for some generous hand to give the vehicle a shove.

But the townsfolk didn't rush forward to push. The foreigner sat helpless behind the glass, without the courage to beg for help. Some time passed. On the face of the international consultant, drops of sweat flowed faster than the slow passing of the minutes.

It was Anna Godwilling who clicked her fingers. In a second, tens of hands joined together at the back of the vehicle. While the townsfolk pushed, the prostitute displayed herself as if she were in a frame, her hands on her thighs. Haughtily, she watched the committee disappear without bothering to wave it goodbye. When the dust settled, she glanced briefly along the road. It was then she saw that Massimo Risi had stayed in the town, along with some of the bigwigs. Anna Godwilling went over to him and said:

—*Thousands of Mozambicans died, and we never got a visit from you then. Now, five foreigners have disappeared and is that the end of the world?*

The Italian remained silent. Anna Godwilling leaned against him flirtatiously, and promised she would help to clear up any mystery. For instance, she could hazard a secret from what she had observed of the victim's remains.

Had the foreigner noticed the size of it? She then proffered the awaited revelation:

    —*That man there was a fully qualified male.*

And the prostitute let out a guffaw while she brushed away some imaginary dust from the long straight tresses of her false hair.

3 A scaly woman

Yearning for a time? I yearn for when there was no time.
(A saying from Tizangara)

The visitors settled down in the town: the minister set himself up in the home of the local administrator. There was another residence for the United Nations representative. But the Italian preferred to put up at the local guesthouse. He wanted to remain independent, away from any schemes organised by the local authorities. I obeyed orders and followed him like a dog. And so I stayed there too, in another room. Next to his, ready for whatever might happen.

Massimo Risi wouldn't allow me to carry his bags and stumbled amongst the potholes in the road, followed by hordes of children begging him for sweets.

—*Masweetie, boss. Masweetie.*

I followed at a respectful distance. But I watched the foreigner: how you could see his soul through his rear end! Europeans, when they walk along, seem to ask the world for permission. They tread the ground delicately but, funnily enough, they make so much noise.

At last we got to the guesthouse. On its front, there were still signs of shooting. The mark of a bullet is like rust: it never grows old. Those little hollows looked so fresh, they even made one tremble, such was the impression that the war was still alive. On a surviving sign over the door were the words 'Jonas Hammer Guesthouse'. Previously, the establishment had been called the 'Hammer and Sickle'. Time and mind wait for no man.

Massimo gingerly entered a gloomy reception hall. A thousand eyes popped and watched the white man going into the guesthouse. In front of a counter covered in old newspapers, the Italian asked:

—*Could you tell me how many stars this establishment has?*

—*Stars?*

The receptionist assumed the man wasn't conversant with good Portuguese and smiled condescendingly:

—*My good sir: at this hour, we haven't any stars here.*

The foreigner turned towards me, asking for help. I stepped forward and explained what the visitor wanted. He wanted to know what the facilities were. The receptionist needed no further encouragement:

—*The facilities? Now that is a complex question because at the present time, the facilities are not the result of forward planning.*

For the rest, there are places where curiosity is not advisable. Stealing a march on time is something that can bring bad luck. And the host advised: let the guest put down his luggage and his soul. When everything was over and done with, and he was about to leave, that would be a good time to become aware of the so-called 'facilities'.

—*Round here, we only know what's happening when it's happened. Do you catch my meaning, dear sir?*

The Italian looked up at the ceiling like a bird seeking a hole in its cage. The question had seemed a silly one to us, but the functionary was prompt in replying to himself:

—*The guesthouse is private, but it belongs to the Party. That is, it belongs to the state.*

And he explained: they nationalised it, then sold it, withdrew its licence, and sold it again. And yet again: they cancelled its ownership and, at that precise time, if the foreigner wanted, the hotelier could even facilitate the paperwork for him to acquire it. He could speak to Jonas, the administrator, who had interests in the business.

—*Do you want to buy the guesthouse?*

—*To buy what?*

—*It's probably going cheap now because it's a very low season for tourists. With all these explosions, there hasn't been much custom ...*

The Italian turned to me as if suddenly burdened by a feeling of remoteness:

—*Could you translate for me afterwards?*

At the receptionist's invitation we followed him down a dark corridor. The man was explaining its shortcomings in the way that a hotelier in any other part of the world would announce the luxuries and comforts of his establishment. And the Italian seemed to regret having ever tried to find things out: there was electricity for only one hour a day.

—*Shit! Have I brought enough batteries?*— he asked himself.

In the end, there was no need for me to translate. Massimo could make himself understood and, what was worse, he understood what was being said to him. The other continued to explain the facilities.

—*There's also no water in the taps.*

—*No water?*

—*Don't worry, my dear sir: first thing in the morning, we'll bring you a can of water.*

—*And where does this water come from?*

—*The water doesn't come from anywhere: it's a boy who brings it.*

We reached the room that had been allotted to the foreigner. I would have the one right next door. I helped the Italian to settle in. The room stank. The hotelier, walking on ahead, was lecturing us on the variety of fauna that inhabited the place: cockroaches, spiders, mice. On the floor, there was a box. The man bent over and started taking things out of it:

—*This magazine is for swatting flies. This old sole is for cockroaches. This walking stick ...*

—*Don't worry, I'll manage.*

The receptionist opened the curtain and a cloud of dust spread through the room. After a while, everything became more visible, but the Italian seemed to prefer the dark. A gooey liquid dribbled down the walls.

—*Is that water?*

—*If only it was, but as I mentioned, we don't have any water here.*

The receptionist was about to leave when he remembered a further recommendation. This time, he directed it to me, as if he were seeking my complicity.

—*From time to time, you know, those insects we call praying mantis get into the room.*

—*Yes, I know what they are.*

—*If you see one, don't kill it*— he said, addressing the Italian now. —*Never do that.*

—*And why not?*

—*Round here, we don't kill those creatures. We have our reasons. He will explain things to you later.*

Risi didn't get as far as sitting down in the solitude of his room. He passed by my room and told me he was going for a walk. He needed some fresh air and hurried off down the corridor. I watched him leave again, and listened to the sound of his steps, as if he were performing the function of a military column all by himself.

Suddenly, the Italian bumped into a shape. It was an old woman, possibly the most aged person he had ever seen. He helped her get up, and led her to the door of the next room. Only then, in the bright light coming through a window, did he notice how loosely wrapped his neighbour's *capulana* was around her wizened frame. The Italian rubbed his eyes as if trying to adjust his vision. It was that the cloth allowed glimpses of a surprisingly smooth body, the flesh of a shapely, seductive young girl. It was as if that wrinkled face did not belong to the substance that was hers.

The Italian quivered. For she was looking at him so seductively that it almost hurt. Even I, who was languidly watching the scene from afar, became alert. The old woman's eyes contained the freshness and saliva of a promised kiss. The woman, all of her, smelled of secretion. Could an old woman of such a great age inspire desire in a man with all his faculties? Massimo Risi hurried to leave. On his way past the reception, he took the opportunity to ask about the ancient woman.

—*Ah! That's Temporina. She only wanders along the corridor and has been living in the dark for centuries.*

—*Doesn't she ever go out?*

—*Go out?! Temporina?!*

The receptionist laughed, but then corrected himself straightaway. Seeing me approach, he chose to address the rest of his speech to me. I drew close, and the Italian and I joined our ears in complicity. Our host pretended to be talking to me secretively, knowing that the other was listening solemnly:

—*Your white friend must be very careful with that old woman.*

—*Why?*— asked Massimo.

—*She's one of those women who go around without taking their shadow with them.*

—*What's he talking about?*— the Italian asked again.

—*You explain things to him in due course.*

We went out. Once in the street, the Italian seemed overcome by the coolness of the afternoon. The market women were clearing up their goods and an immense peace seemed to be returning to the inner recesses of things. Risi sat down in the only bar in town. He seemed to want to be alone and I respected his wish. I sat myself down further away, enjoying my dose of fresh air. People passed by and greeted the foreigner in a friendly manner. Many minutes went by and I asked him whether he wanted to return to the guesthouse. He didn't want to. He didn't feel like doing anything except to stay where he was, away from his room and far from his duties. I sat down next to him. He looked at me as if for the first time:

—*Who are you?*

—*I'm your translator.*

—*I can speak and understand. The problem isn't the language. What I don't understand is this world here.*

An invisible weight caused his head to droop. He seemed defeated, without hope.

—*I have to complete this mission. All I want is my long overdue promotion.*

—*You'll get it.*

—*Do you think I'm going to find out who made the soldiers explode?*

The Italian was all of a tatter. His sparse hair was dishevelled. At that point a man in rags appeared and introduced himself:

—*I'm sorry, my bosses. I wish to speak to this foreigner from elsewhere.*

—*What's the matter?*

—*It's that I'm linked to the deceased.*

—*The deceased?!*

—*The goat that was trodden on by the car.*

—*So what?*

—*It's that I'm the owner of that selfsame goat. Now, who is going to pay me damages?*

And he rubbed his fingers together, as if suggesting the tinkling of money. Fortunately, the Italian didn't understand what was happening. I asked the owner of the unfortunate goat to come back later. He was walking off when suddenly he remembered something and turned back. To my astonishment, he announced that my father had arrived in town. I didn't believe him at first.

—*He's arrived. And he's gone to live in his old house.*

I was surprised. He who had announced that he would never return to Tizangara. Now that I was involved in this mission, and obliged to live in the guesthouse, now he decided to reinstall himself in my childhood home!

The Italian sensed my concern.

—*What's happening?*

—*You don't know what it means to have my old man back.*

Without being aware of it, I was opening myself up and confessing ancient memories to the foreigner. The advantage of having a stranger listen to us is that we confide in him the lie that we have only one soul.

4 *Introducing the teller of the tale*

> *God gave me the task of dying.*
> *I didn't carry it out.*
> *But now, I've learned how to obey.*
> (Words of Dona Hortensia)

There are those who are born with a defect. I was born out of a defect. Let me explain: at my birth, they failed to extract all of me, completely. Part of me remained there, stuck to my mother's insides. This was such that she couldn't see me: she looked and didn't catch sight of me. That part of me that remained inside her stole me away from her field of vision. She couldn't accept this:

—*You are out of my sight, but I shall find a way of seeing you!*

Such is life: a live fish, but that only lives in the flow of water. Whoever wants to capture this fish must kill it. Only then can it be possessed. I speak of time, and I speak of water. Our children are like flowing water, the irretrievable course of time. Has a river got a date of birth? On what precise day are our children born?

My mother's advice consisted merely of silences. She spoke with the accent of a cloud.

—*It's life that is the most contagious thing*— she would say.

I would ask her to explain our destiny, anchored as we were in poverty.

—*See there, my son, you've picked up the concerns of the whites!*— She would incline her head as if her head were fleeing from her thought, and she would warn me: —*You seek to understand the world, which is something beyond our understanding.*

And in a graver tone, she would point out:

—*The idea perches on you like a snipe: with only one leg. So as not to weigh too heavily on your heart.*

—*Honestly, mother …*

—*For the heart, my son, the heart always has a different thought.*

Such was her talk, nearer her mouth than her brain. Once, she pulled me over to sit down next to her. She had a solemn air about her. And she said:

—*Yesterday, I had something that might have been a thought.*

—*What did you think?*

—*It was more or less this: I didn't need to be alive in order to see you. Do you understand me?*

While she spoke, her fingers typed my face, line by line. My mother read me through twisted fingers.

—*You are like me.*

After me, her belly closed up. I wasn't just her son – I

was her punishment for being unable to be a mother again. And that fate multiplied itself in other forms of punishment: my father, instead of showering her with greater affection, began to inflict further pain on her, blaming her for all the misfortunes of the world. And that made him feel relief: if she had lost her fertility, he had a right to abandon his duties.

—*Now I'm not liable for anything. I can unrestrain myself.*

And he began to spend nights away, spending his age in other women's beds. My mother wept while sleeping in the unconjugal solitude of her bed. She didn't sob, nor did the outpouring of her sadness lend itself to be heard. Only tears rolled ceaselessly down her cheeks all night long. So that she awoke drenched in a pool of the purest, most distilled water. I would help her from there, from those waters, and always dry her with the same cloth. It could never be with another towel: that was the cloth that had been used for her only birth. That cloth had swaddled me at the morning of my existence. Who knows, it might be her shroud.

In spite of my mother's nocturnal sadness, I lived as peacefully as a fish in still water. At that time, there were no days of old. For me, everything was recent, in the process of being born. In certain months I would help my mother on our allotment. I would accompany her along paths that were always new, such was the greenery that kept reoccupying the spaces. She would smile, as if excusing the forest for its bad manners:

—*Round here, the bush loves to grow.*

In the spaces between the crops, my mother would sit

down, under the rustling leaves of the marula tree. She would hold my hand as she spoke. And she would gradually unpick her sorrows: our tradition doesn't permit a child to be present at a funeral. Death is reserved for grown-ups to see. Only it seemed that my mother, already a grown woman, was not authorised to see my own life. And she concluded, as if in agreement with herself:

—*Life, my son, is a disillusionist.*

As the afternoon drew to an end, the flamingos would cross the sky. My mother fell silent as she watched their flight. She wouldn't utter a word until those tall birds had been lost from sight. Nor could I move. Everything at that moment was sacred. As the light faded, my mother, in a low voice, would sing a song that she had drawn from her invention. For her, it was the flamingos that pushed the sun so that day could begin on the other side of the world.

—*This spot is for them to come back to again tomorrow!*

Once, we agreed a pact, with God as our witness. We made promises, sanctified by spells: that I would visit her the moment she was taking leave of life. For in the space of that very instant, she believed she would finally be able to see my face and body. And so it was agreed: when she entered her moribund state, she would let me know. I would rush to her, and she would at last get to know me eye to eye.

Time went by and I left the area, encouraged by Father Muhando. In the city, I was able to go and attend classes. School, for me, was like a ship: it gave me access to other worlds. But education didn't make me complete. On the contrary: the more I learned, the more stifled I was. And I spent a good few years gaining precise and precious knowledge.

On the return journey, it would no longer be me who was returning. It would be someone I didn't know, without my childhood. No one's fault. Just this: I'm a tree born on a shore. Further over there, in the distance, I'm a dugout, swept away by the current; nearer in, I'm a piece of timber unable to escape the fire.

One day, the time for my old mother's oath to be carried out arrived. I received an urgent summons: my mother was letting go of her soul. I travelled on the back of an old truck. On arriving at the town, I rushed home in the blinking of an eye. I had to get there before she divested herself of the world. Did I arrive late? In a mother's old heart, her children always return too late. She seized my hand and closed her eyes as if she were breathing through them. She was so still, so without movement in her breast, that I got worried. The others calmed me down:

—*She's just pretending to be dead. Just so that God will have pity on her.*

But it was no pretence. No one realised that she, as a result of her fainting, had finally caught sight of me. She was focussing on me and all my congruities. Her face creased in an illegible smile:

—*After all, you look like him …*

—*Like my father?*

She smiled once more, a smile that was almost a sigh, while she repeated:

—*Like him …*

She squeezed my hand, in a spasm. Her eyelid had

already turned to stone. Death is the narrowest of balconies. From it, one glimpses time like an eagle hovering over a cliff – and round about all space can turn into a splendid flight of fancy.

—*Mother? Who is he?*

I asked her this so as to give the impression that I had not noticed that she was no longer alive. I was trying to attenuate my sadness. I sat there with my mother's body leaning lightly against my chest, as if it were a recently fallen baobab leaf. She had died the very instant she had begun her contemplation of me. Could it be true that she had at last seen me? I didn't attach importance even to that. What I needed to do was to get word of what had happened to my father.

Our folk don't live without paying great attention to the welfare of those who have passed beyond, westwards. Our custom is like this: life is to the east, death to the west. Death, and all its inexplicable uses! My mother had departed on the curve of the rain, to go and inhabit an unglittering star. From then on, life no longer appeared to her: she had achieved the ultimate disencounter. I still recall her words that nourished a hope for me at a time when I had lost all faith:

—*Don't you see those rivers that never fill the sea? Our lives are like that too: everything is still to live for.*

And now, fortuitously, I was setting off to look for my father. Where was he hanging about? Was he still there on the edge of our district, incapable of distance, unsuited to proximity? Did he still rent his old boat from the fishermen at the mouth of the river? I hoped so, for I had grown attached to that little boat, the times that I had been left in my father's care. It was I who had named the craft: *Rainboat*. And I would stand at the prow, as it bobbed along through the waves of those waters. When the dam was built, the river became milder and the estuary gentler, making it possible for craft to navigate its waters all year round.

Every time I visited my father I joined in the lives of those folk. I helped with the fishing, I hauled in the net, speared octopus, tied up the boat. My father would greet me contentedly on the beach. He never wanted to know whether I was tired or not. He had his own clear ideas about work. For him, it was the boat that made the oars go along. During his whole life, he had only ever lived inland. He was knowledgeable about the bush, but ignorant in matters of the ocean.

In those days, my body was still full of life, and open to all manner of beliefs and beginnings. At night, before the crackling fire, old Sulpício would ask me to tell him my watery adventures. He would smile, justifying his inabilities in marine matters:

—*A shrimp moves around in the water and yet can't swim.*

After the disagreements he had had with the administration, my old man didn't have a good word to say about work. Before, he had believed in the power of toil to create a future. He had lost that belief. Only a year or two previously, he had even decided to wear pyjamas for the rest of his life. Only at night time, when his pyjamas should have performed their congenital function, did he take them off. He took his pyjamas off in order to sleep.

—*But father, why do you wear pyjamas during the day?*

The thing was that he would have a snooze here and there, sometimes lying down in the brightest light. And so, in such dress, he was well prepared for the occasional forty winks. But pyjamas weren't the only matter: the old man accumulated obsessions that ran counter to universal habit. Such as in the following example: he only wore shoes on Sundays. On the other days of the week, his feet hugged the earth, happy to stroke the ground in all its infinity. At the end of the day, he would pour warm tea over his legs. His bare feet would soak in a bowl, enjoying their restful bath.

—*I'm giving them a drink*— and he would laugh.

Such eccentric behaviour would irritate my old lady. But his strangeness had its explanation: he walked around barefoot in order not to wear out his only pair of shoes. He carried them dangling from his hands, but without ever putting them on while he was walking. He would only put them on afterwards, when he stopped, and struck his gentlemanly pose.

Those moments in the company of my old man pulled me in the direction of uncertain dreams, who knows, maybe that sense of peace was what they call tenderness. Those fleeting times, I now realise, were my only home. On the estuary where my old man abdicated from his existence, I invented my own source.

Yet the visits to the river mouth were brief and few, mere flashes in my memory. In the end, my mother forbade his negative influences on me. My old man had to pay for his irresponsibility with isolation. She was getting her revenge for his desertion. When he left the family, for some time he still drifted around the vicinity. Then, he settled on the outskirts of town, making of his life what we do with a bed sheet: we fold it and tuck it under the mattress. We never glimpsed the tucks in his life, or the direction his existence was taking. This was a mystery that lay concealed under itself. He only began to appear again when I was already a young lad. And he began to visit us from time to time. He would stay for a day or two. I never noticed which room he slept in. Deep down, I wanted to preserve the illusion that he and my mother still shared their nights under one roof.

The next morning, he would lead me through a piece of waste ground. He wouldn't go very far. There, next to a huge termite hill, he would pause. He would crouch down next to the ground and stroke the nest. Then, he would get up and point beyond the leafy bulk of some silver terminalia trees:

—*Can you see that little path?*

All I could see was foliage. The savannah there was covered in different tones of green. It was no use looking too closely. We were both too scared to go any further. But he pointed into the distance and insisted on his warning:

—*When the end of the world comes, you take that little track. Do you hear me?*

That was advice I never wanted to take. But I could never doubt his word. That he knew he was right and that humanity would come to an end for sure.

All this I remembered when I arrived at Inhamudzi beach, where my old man had exiled himself. It wasn't far away and I had travelled more memories than kilometres.

This time, I was almost removed from myself, as if life had disqualified me. What use was my city knowledge? Those paths had uses that were not the same as city streets: they seemed to have been made solely for dreams and sunsets to travel along.

Those narrow little tracks alleviated the land's sadness, allowing access for the last rays of the sun to light the secret recesses of our soul. I wandered through the area, I looked among the shacks and grass hovels. There was no sign of him, only sayings, rumours, this and that. Did old Sulplício know his own reality?

Then finally I found him. What had become of my father? He was skinny, vacant, as if his soul were something outside him. Since my last visit, he had become the tenant in the dark hollow of an old lighthouse. He had become a lighthouse keeper. He had risen to occupy a disused lighthouse, for no ship used that route out to sea anymore.

The old man, however, took his new profession seriously. It required a lot of attention: focussing on the infinite, surveying the horizon. Hadn't he spent his whole life inspecting and guarding the savannah?! Now, he was merely changing the object of his vigilance. It must have been because of this that he pretended I was invisible when I spoke:

—*Father, I bring sad news from Tizangara.*

With a firm gesture he bade me remain silent. He was concentrating on the wind speed. He glanced at the horizon and shook his head:

—*Do you remember how I was learning the language of the birds? Well, your mother never let me.*

—*Father, listen to me ...*

—*Nowadays, son, I don't speak any language, only dialects. Do you understand?*

I didn't understand anything. My father wandered without any structure to his thoughts. My serious air, insisting on the matter that had brought me there, soon annoyed him.

—*You remind me of your mother: you never understand. How irritating that is!*

For the rest, he refused to listen. He waved his hand categorically, severing my speech from me.

—*Go back there, I don't want to hear anything you have to say ...*

—*But father, mother ...*

—*I don't want to hear ...*

I listened to his steps as he climbed the spiral staircase. Suddenly, he stopped. His voice reached me, distorted:

—*It's strange. You don't hear the sound of gunshot here!*

—*Father, the war's over.*

—*Do you believe that?*

I was already on my way back, when his voice hovered over me. He was speaking from the window high up in the tower.

—*Do you remember the little track behind our house? Well, don't forget: if the world comes to an end suddenly, you follow that path.*

5   Temporina's explanation

Some people know and don't believe.
These never manage to see.
Others don't know and believe.
These don't see more than a blind man.
(Proverb from Tizangara)

The Italian had reclined as flat as a clock hand. He seemed to have enjoyed the story of my childhood. When I finished, he lay there in silence. For a time he remained like that, at one with the pause. Only after a while did he speak:

—*This story of yours ... is it all true?*

—*What do you mean, true?*

—*Forgive my asking. But my mind wandered as I lay here listening. What time is it?*

It was time for us to go back to the guesthouse. A razor-sharp wind was blowing. The same receptionist was at the entrance, sweeping up some bits of plastic. Some of the letters from the sign had fallen off in the wind. Now it read: 'Jo Hammer'.

The Italian was tired and wasn't even conscious of falling asleep. That night, he was gripped by a strange dream: the old woman from the corridor came into his room and undressed, revealing the most appetising flesh he had ever set eyes on. In his dream, the Italian made love to her. Never in his life had Massimo Risi experienced such delicious caresses. He rolled this way and that between the sheets, groaning loudly and rubbing himself against the pillow. If this was a nightmare, he was certainly enjoying himself.

He woke up sweating and dirty, his chest still heaving. He looked around him and noticed that someone had been rummaging in his clothes. Someone had been in his room. He got up and saw the bucket of water. He sighed, relieved. It had been the receptionist for sure. Massimo washed himself with the help of a glass. He shaved with the water left over from his washing. He stood looking at the bucket as if for the first time noticing how much a bit of water is worth. Then he left the room and sneaked off down the corridor, when suddenly, an arm held him back. It was the old woman, Temporina. The Italian stopped in his tracks, icy with fear. The old woman coyly took a few steps round the foreigner. Then she leaned flirtatiously against the door of the room. She gave a strange smile as she pointed to her stomach:

—*I'm pregnant by you ...*

Risi asked in a faint voice:

—*What?*

—*Last night, you made me pregnant.*

The man was dumbfounded. The old woman smiled, ran

her finger over the foreigner's lips and went back into the room, closing the door behind her. Risi lingered in the corridor before returning to his room. He sat on the edge of his bed while memories of the dream came back to him. Then he noticed a *capulana* on the floor! How had it got there? A knock on the door caused him to rush over and hide the suspicious piece of cloth under the bed. It was the receptionist who came in, full of formalities. After a succession of 'if you pleases', he got to the point:

—*Senhor Massimo, I heard everything.*

—*What everything?*

—*What happened out there in the corridor.*

My heart missed a beat. If word got around that the Italian was involved with Temporina, the affair would become the talk of the town among the inhabitants of Tizangara. The receptionist didn't seem to care about such rumours. Which was why he pressed Massimo Risi:

—*Take care, my friend. That woman's bewitched. Who knows whether you won't explode like the others?*

—*But I didn't do anything.*

—*Yet she claims you made her pregnant! Unless, of course, she's the second Virgin Mary ...*

—*I swear I never touched that woman*— the Italian protested.

—*Now the girl's going to want to go back with you to your country. She and her mulatto child.*

A certain scorn was discernible in the way he said 'mulatto'. Father Muhando had spoken out about this kind of prejudice. The priest's thought got straight to the heart of the matter: aren't we all mulattos? But the people of

Tizangara didn't want to acknowledge their mixture. For to be black — to be of that race — had been inculcated in us as being our one and only source of pride. And some of us created our identity in this illusory mirror.

Massimo looked distracted. Was he trying to work out in his mind how such an unforeseen succession of events had affected his life?

—*I just can't understand it!*

—*I know, it's hard. And all the more so because that woman doesn't actually exist.*

—*She doesn't exist?*

—*She doesn't exist in the way you think.*

—*What do you mean by that?*

I was already listening to this conversation from the corridor. I decided to go in. The receptionist heaved a sigh of relief and pointing at me, said:

—*Let him explain. And take my advice, the best thing you can do is grab that walking stick and beat her with it. That's the only way you'll get her out of your dreams.*

And the receptionist was on the point of leaving when he noticed something on the floor. He bent down to take a closer look and exclaimed in a high-pitched voice:

—*You've killed her!*

The Italian jumped up anxiously. Another death? And the receptionist, holding his head in his hands, shouted as he gazed at the floor:

—*Hortensia!*

The Italian went from normal to astonished without stopping at surprised. Hortensia? What was happening now? He looked at me as if asking for my help, and I walked over to the receptionist for an explanation. The man was pointing at a dead praying mantis on the floor. I felt a shiver run through me too. All of a sudden, that dead body was something more than an insect. The receptionist went on in a mournful tone:

—*It was always around here, in the rooms.*

He couldn't have been sadder. Once the Italian had understood, he tried to get rid of the receptionist. He no longer had any reserves of patience at all. And with the walking stick, he pushed the insect out of the room, sweeping it away as if it were a mere piece of trash.

—*Now then, explain. What in heaven's name is this all about?*

A praying mantis wasn't just any old insect. It was an ancestor visiting the living. I explained this belief to Massimo: the creature had gone there at the bidding of a dead man. Killing it could be a bad omen. The Italian looked at the stick and propped it in a corner of the room. He was lost in concentration. Yet he didn't even seem to be thinking about the matter. His look revealed that it wasn't a mantis but a woman occupying his thoughts.

I sat down on the bedside table and decided to uncover the mystery surrounding Temporina. Not by myself. That afternoon, without saying a word, I went and called the old woman while Massimo lay sprawled on his bed. He was too tired to do any cleaning up, to check to see whether there were any creepy-crawlies on the mattress. He let his mind wander. His senses would have exiled themselves from him if it weren't for a gentle voice:

—*Don't be scared. It's me.*

It was Temporina, his aged neighbour. She lingered in the shadows, leaning in a corner.

—*I've brought you something to drink.*

And she offered him a glass. The Italian half raised himself in the bed and took the drink.

—*So what's this, then?*

—*Don't ask. Drink it, and don't be frightened.*

He swallowed the drink in one go. Temporina even tried to stop him from doing this, but to no avail. She wanted him to pour a few drops on the floor, by way of homage to the departed. In this case, Hortensia. The Italian smacked his lips. The false old woman approached the light. Her body glowed while the Italian discreetly apprised himself of the woman's beauty. Only then did I speak:

—*Temporina, explain who you are. And you, my Italian friend, listen carefully.*

Temporina leaned against the chest of drawers, while her gaze exceeded her look. A strange smile dominated her face. It was like that happiness I had already seen in the faces of the old: the mere fact of dying later, after time has stopped. And she spoke in her young girl's voice:

—*I have two ages. But I'm a little girl. I'm not even twenty.*

—*Holy Mother of God!*— sighed Massimo, shaking his head.

—*I've got an old woman's face because I was punished by the spirits.*

—*Holy Mother of God!*— the Italian repeated.

—*They punished me because times had gone by without any man tasting my flesh.*

I helped explain. I knew Temporina, she was only a bit older than me. It was true: she had never accepted any suitor as a young girl. Before she knew it, she was no longer a teenager. Over the hill. And that's how divine punishment descended upon her. In the space of just one night, her face filled with wrinkles, as time redesigned itself in her. But the rest of her body preserved its youth.

—*Come with me. I want to show you something.*

Temporina tugged at the foreigner and pushed him along the corridor to the reception. Then, cautious, she stopped.

—*You go in front. No one can see me going out just like that. Otherwise they'll make me leave the guesthouse.*

The Italian glanced back and insisted I went with him. Deep down, he was afraid of Temporina. In a curt tone, he ordered:

—*Come with us.*

Temporina led us along a darkened alley. I knew what we would find. I was familiar with the route, and knew where we were going. I lingered at the back so that the European might see for himself what would follow. We were on our way to the house of Dona Hortensia, Temporina's aunt. So we were going to meet the deceased Hortensia. The woman who, according to the receptionist, visited the guesthouse in the form of a praying mantis. And who perhaps visited the living in other forms too. For she was the deadest creature in all Tizangara. Hortensia was the youngest granddaughter of the founders of the town.

—*Where are we going? I don't want to go any further. I'm going back to the guesthouse.*

The Italian had suddenly awoken to the reality of his situation. And he stopped in the middle of the path. Temporina turned back and urged him:

—*Come on! We're going to the house of my late aunt.*

Massimo still refused. He wanted to go back to the guesthouse and concentrate on matters concerning his investigation.

I helped Temporina to reassure the foreigner. Hortensia's home was important for his mission. The big old house had been used to accommodate the United Nations soldiers. It was the administrator who had taken that decision against everyone's wish. The house was a place of spirits. It didn't matter what the soldiers did. What did matter was what the place would do to unauthorised visitors.

—*You may even find documents, evidence left behind by the soldiers.*

Massimo hesitated and then accepted. We arrived, but didn't go inside straightaway. We sat down by the front door. The foreigner, seeing me with my eyes closed, thought I was praying. But I was just conjuring up sweet memories of the dead woman. And I was letting time occupy my mind.

At the entrance, Temporina called:

—*Can we come in, Aunt Hortensia?*

Silence. The Italian gripped my shoulder: wasn't Hortensia dead? One had to ask a dead person's permission? I asked him to respect the silence. At a barely noticeable sign, Temporina got an answer from the former proprietor. We could go in. Once again, the Italian baulked. So I told him the old lady's story.

Hortensia. It was no coincidence that she had the name of a flower. Not because she was pretty. But she would sit the whole day on the veranda, pretending to watch time go by. It wasn't upon time that she focussed her gaze. For it would be true to say that she had gained access to other visions.

Aunt Hortensia lived with her nephew and niece. Temporina was the elder. The nephew was a boy of proven disabilities. The lad was slow and dopey, as retarded in his mind as he was in his movements. His head had never been visited by a single idea and he lived at peace with himself, as satisfied as a saint after committing a sin. The lad wasn't a what's-his-name, nor an individual, which was why he had never been given a name. Was it worth wasting a human name on a creature with questionable faculties? All Hortensia did was to display herself on the veranda. That was the stage she performed on throughout the day.

—*But Auntie, why do you veranda yourself so much, from morning till night?*

—*I just want to be viewable.*

So perhaps it was vanity that summoned her to the veranda, dressed in the most beautiful cloth and with her hair kept in place by a kerchief. Aunt Hortensia was single and no one knew any stories about her. No man had ever laid his head on her pillow. For sure, no man had ever been granted a visa to her heart. She sat on the veranda just as folk had always known her: her soul admitted no traffic through it, for there was no space for parking. Who would end up with the old spinster's wealth? the townsfolk asked themselves. She hadn't been legged over, but at least she was worth a legacy.

—*The day I stop having a bath.*

That was her way of saying when she would die. She spoke in elaborate images. For on that day, Hortensia would say, when she had finally retired behind her eyelids, they would come and take away her goods and chattels, empty her house to the point where it would be like their empty recollection of her. Her withdrawal from the world of the living began to occupy her thoughts excessively. Every little thing was an excuse for leave-taking. She was profligate in her farewells. If she left the room to go to the lavatory or to the kitchen, she would do so with all due ceremony. As if rehearsing the final departure.

When at last illness began to dispute her body, Hortensia called for her nephew and niece, and addressed Temporina:

—*I'm not leaving you anything, little niece. It's not worth it: these possessions of mine will die of sadness without me. No one else will be their owner*— and turning to her nephew: —*You take everything. You, my little nephew, are such a simpleton that you won't even realise that these objects, my assets, will evaporate, ground into such a fine dust that not the slightest trace of them will be left. Do you understand, nephew?*

The young lad shook his head clumsily. She explained again, using shorter words. As she had never had a man love her, she had allowed the objects to fall in love with her. Her possessions would therefore commit suicide if they were deprived of her company.

—*And now you can leave, my brainless little nephew.*

The two women were left alone. At that point her aunt seized both her hands and spoke to her. She should take care. She should surrender herself to the arms of a man without delay. Otherwise, she would follow in her poor aunt's footsteps. Or worse still, the punishment of old age might descend upon her, pretty as she was.

—*Now, my girl, take me out on to the veranda.*

Temporina carried her out into the stillness of the night. She sat down in the old armchair and sighed as she looked out on to the street. Just a few people could be seen making their way to the church.

—*Do you want to know why I've always sat on the veranda?*

—*And why was that, Aunt Hortensia?*

—*To see if God would pick me out and carry me off. He never did. I'm very dark-skinned, so it must be because of that. He never chose me even though I've sat here, right in front of the church.*

Hortensia crossed over into the shadows that very night. She died holding her niece's hand. They say it was their closeness that caused the curse of solitude to pass from Hortensia to Temporina. That was why the girl had been spinstered up until now.

I opened my eyes again. Recollection of all these things was now so intense that it was as if no time had passed at all. There was I, revisiting memories, running the risk of awakening ghosts. Yet my mission was to accompany Massimo Risi. Only this authorised me to intrude into the world of Aunt Hortensia. And something I had said had encouraged the Italian official to come with me.

The Italian immediately began to rummage around. He was looking for some vestige of the soldiers' presence. There was hardly anything. Everything was disposed as if Hortensia still lived there. The Italian, whether out of respect or fear, merely brushed the surface of things.

—*Help me*— he asked.

However, the afternoon was already in decline, and there was only a lingering trace of light. I walked along a corridor and soon got a soul-chilling fright. A skinny boy, like a ghost, burst out of one of the rooms. It was Temporina's crazy brother. She got up and tidied her brother's shirt. That was her way of greeting him silently. The boy made a vague gesture, placing one hand over his head and pointing at the Italian.

—*He would like a cap, one of those blue ones like yours. He wants to be a soldier, one of yours ...*

The Italian smiled, without uttering a word. The young boy returned, shadowlike, to his darkened world. We stood there in silence, as if we'd just received news of a death. In the town, we all knew that it was Hortensia who continued to look after her nephew. Every morning, a plate of food appeared on the table. The boy would sit down, lonely and mute. He would eat slowly, his eyes fixed on a particular point. At the end of the meal, he would always repeat the same words: *Thank you, Auntie.*

We told the foreigner about this attention. He gave a strange smile. Temporina broke the silence and asked the Italian:

—*Sit down over there in that armchair. You can go on looking tomorrow.*

Massimo obeyed. From where he sat, he could hear the humdrum noises of the town. In some corners, bonfires cast irregular light upon the houses. Further away, the generator lit up the administration building and Estêvão Jonas's residence.

—*This town has been swallowed up by the bush.*

I looked around me and agreed with the girl. The town had been gradually abandoned, so much so that things were losing their name. Over there, for example, that was once called a house. Now, with roots filling its ruined walls, it would better be described as a tree.

—*Do you now understand why we came here? For you to see that in Tizangara, there aren't two worlds.*

Let him see for himself the living and the dead sharing the same house. Like Hortensia and her nephew. And he should think about that as he searched for his dead.

—*That's why I'm asking you, Massimo: which town is it you are visiting?*

—*What do you mean by which town?*

—*It's just that we have three towns, each with their respective names – Tizangara-land, Tizangara-sky, Tizangara-water. I know all three. And I'm the only one here who loves them all.*

I smiled. Now it was I who needed a translator. I had never heard Temporina so awash with beauty. Or was she putting it on especially for the visitor? I had my suspicions and tiptoed away down the stairs. I left the two of them on the veranda while I remained in the yard at a discreet distance. From where I was, I could still see how Temporina sat on the Italian's lap and how their bodies were entwined.

Suddenly, the light caught her face and I was dumbstruck: in the act of love, Temporina was rejuvenating. She displayed no wrinkles, none of the scars of time. I looked away, withdrew into my modesty. The Italian would come downstairs and I would resume my duties. But for the time being, he didn't need a translator, that was plain to see.

While I waited, I fell asleep. The following day, when I woke up, the Italian was already strolling round the garden. Temporina was talking to him:

—*I've been watching you. I'm sorry, Massimo, but you don't know how to walk.*

—*What do you mean, don't know how to walk?*

—*You don't know how to tread. You don't know how to walk on this ground. Come here: I'll show you how to walk.*

He laughed, thinking it was a joke. But she warned him solemnly:

—*I'm talking seriously: knowing how to tread this ground is the difference between life and death. Come, and I'll teach you.*

The Italian complied. They stood together hand in hand. They looked as if they were dancing, the Italian lightening his weight as his foot got used to the ground. Temporina encouraged him as they went along: tread like someone in love, tread as if you were stepping on a woman's breast. And she led him with a nudge and a gesture. Further away, her simpleton brother nervously stifled his laugh. He jumped and leaped, goatlike. He had never seen his sister in womanly pursuits. Later, I would discover that there were other reasons for his nervousness.

Temporina withdrew at last, and the Italian allowed

himself to fall into a shadow. I know white people: Risi's gaze showed that he had been smitten by passion. The spell had already taken hold of the foreigner. The poor man was ignorant of all that awaited him. And so it was that, smiling ingenuously, he came over to me. I teased him:

—*Did you tousle your hair well and truly with Temporina last night?*

The foreigner was slow to understand. He asked me to explain. I just laughed.

—*Do you think I touched that woman?*

—*I don't think: I saw you!*

—*Well, I can swear I didn't lay a finger on her.*

The Italian was adamant. It was as if he felt a need to banish any doubt from my mind. He explained that after I had left them, they had talked. And that he had fallen asleep. Yes, he admitted he had dreamed of the old-young girl. But nothing had happened.

We were interrupted by a call from the direction of the front gate. It was a messenger from the administration. He handed me an envelope.

—*It's a letter from His Excellency*— then he came closer to confide in me: —*He says you should read it first. And only translate a summary of it for the foreigner.*

I didn't follow these instructions. I waited for the messenger to leave and sat down in the shade. I read the entire letter out loud to Massimo Risi.

6 The administrator's first epistle

I'm not a bad recollector.
My only difficulty
is having to write things down in writing.
(The administrator's confession)

His Excellency
The Provincial Governor

I am writing, Excellency, almost by mouth. The things I shall narrate, which happened here in this locality, are worthy of such astonishment that they are hardly suitable for an official report. Take this report as if it were a letter from a family friend. Forgive this abuse of formality.

It all began in the early hours of the morning before last. My wife, Dona Ermelinda, came to the window and asked what all the noise was about. I opened my sluggish eyes with difficulty and saw her shoulders tremble, all of a quiver. She curled up inside her capulana; *it was as if there was an invisible chill. I all but snorted, for it was hardly a noise. Ermelinda often makes me lose my patience: it's because my wife, Excellency, sleeps with her ears on the outside, sniffing away like a hyena, always on the prowl. She suffers from fears both within and outside her sleep. On this occasion, she was whineful and persistent:*

—Can't you hear, Jonas? It's like a ship's siren …

I untangled myself from the sheets and cursed my luck. It seemed to me she'd heard thunder up in the sky. Ermelinda opened the heavy curtains inherited from the colonials. We both looked out. Outside, the day was still rising, grey and languid.

Begging your pardon, but sincerity isn't sinful: praise be to Marxism, but there's a lot out there hidden away in those African silences. Underneath the material basis of the world, there must be artisan forces we can't even account for. I'm sorry if I'm mistaken, but I'm just giving you the benefit of my self-criticism.

Let me return to the story. Looking through the window, I then noticed the strangest thing: there wasn't any wind or a single cloud. The place was calm and in peaceful order. But further over, the river was kicking and struggling like hell itself. How could that be: calm over here but agitated over there? What forces were they that ill disposed the world on one side alone? Where were those rumblings of thunder coming from? Ermelinda asked me anxiously:

—And the drum-dancing?

—What drum-dancing, comrade wife?

Note, Your Excellency, the due respect I show when addressing a Mozambican woman. We leaders have to provide an example within the very heart of the family. Ermelinda's nerves were on edge and she continued to press me:

—Didn't you hear the people stamping their feet to the beat of the drums? What ceremony could it be?

The truth of the matter was that the drums had been beating all night long pandemonically.

—Why did you allow these people to get so near?

I, Estêvão Jonas, lost my temper. She wasn't to interfere. Those people, she knew only too well, were one-time war refugees. The conflict was over, but they hadn't gone back to the countryside. Ermelinda is aware of both the current and former orientations. In the old days, they would have been packed off far away. That was what used to happen when there were visiting dignitaries, cadres and foreigners. We had instructions from above: we couldn't show the nation to be begging, the country with its ribcage on show. On the day before any visit, all of us administrators would get an urgent order: we were to hide the population, sweep all the misery away.

However, with donations from the international community, things had changed. Now the situation was quite the opposite. We needed to show the population off in all its hunger and with all its contagious diseases. I can clearly recall your words, Excellency: our destitution is turning a good profit. To live in a country of beggars, it is necessary to uncover our sores, expose the protruding bones of our children. Those were the words of your speech, and I even jotted them down in my notebook. This is the current order of the day: gather together your remains, make it easier for the disaster to be seen. The foreigner from outside, or from the capital, should be able to appreciate all the wretchedness without sweating about it too much. That's why these refugees have been camping in the vicinity of the administration building for the last six months, giving themselves airs of misfortune.

—Can't you hear it now? Over there, it's a ship weeping ...

My wife, Excellency, is just too obstinate! Ships haven't come up as far as Tizangara for over a century. The river here no longer gets any visitors. So how could she have heard a ship? That's why I decided to take charge of the situation. I shouted for the guard. He appeared, all full of salutes. He was so sleepy that, at first, he spoke in Chimuanzi. I had indeed received Your Excellency's recommendation: learning the local language facilitates understanding with the people. But I haven't been able to, I don't even have time for priorities. There was the guard standing like a statue, his hands next to his body. I issued my command: the noises had to stop right away.

—But what noises, Excellency?

—Those drums, can't you even hear?

—But Mister Diministrator, sir, don't you know our ceremonies? It's our mass, up here in the North.

—I don't want to know— *I answered.*

I was authority, I couldn't stand there making small talk. It wasn't worth continuing the dialogue: he was a local, just like the others, with a scallywag's tendencies. That was why the noise was music to him.

The guard went out, his ankles before his feet. Ermelinda gave a deep sigh. She's been complaining about me for some time. She says all I do is grumble, as if I was carrying the lid of my own coffin around with me. The problem, according to her, is that I make myself bigger than my size. According to her complaints, she sees me as an ox looking at a swollen toad: no matter how great the inflation, its ribs are always visible. To which I answer: you don't know, woman, you don't know anything at all. Ermelinda doesn't even listen to me, she just goes on and on:

—You should be like those little birds that live on the hippo's back. Make yourself needed but without anyone seeing you.

Her bragging gets on my nerves. If she's so clever, then why isn't she the administrator? Or the administratess? I always remind her of my status as a hero from the armed struggle. Out there in the bush, without anything to eat. All out of a spirit of sacrifice to free the people. Once I even had only Colgate to eat.

—Well, you should have eaten more toothpaste! Your breath still stinks.

See how she answers back, tit-for-tat. But on that occasion, my wife had no effect on me. Her voice even gained a sweet concern:

—Husband, watch your heart.

—What's the matter with it?

—It's growing bigger than your chest, Jonas.

Cupping her hand, she held it out and touched me. And do you know where she touched me, Excellency? On my breast, she stroked my breast. And she asked me:

—Don't you see, husband? Look how you're palpitating, you'll do yourself some harm. When the blood boils, Jonas, it must be for other reasons. Or isn't that so, husband?

I softened, full of breath. My breast, Excellency, is the point where the beast in me is untied, like that little button that switches on the radio. I smiled. I should have allowed my body to do what it could, and take my fill of her caramel sweetness. But I was hollow, deep in thoughts travelling far and wide. Ermelinda still waited a while. But then she lost her temper and burst out:

—You're thinking about that other woman!

—No, I'm not. I promise— *I answered firmly.*

I drew close to her to try and undo her suspicions. Ermelinda resisted at first. Then she sweetened, and paid me a little warmth. And running her hand down my chest, we both laughed and fell into bed. Forgive me, Excellency, I'm getting away from politics, which is the subject of our common interest.

I'm going to interrupt this report because my sap is beginning to rise. I only have to remember it for my liquids to boil. I've never confessed this to you before, and you will certainly tease me for it. It's just that whenever I touch a woman, my hands heat up until they're like red-hot coals. There have been times when they've even caught fire and I've had to stop in the middle of the act. Can you imagine such a thing? It must be a spell that Ermelinda has cast on me. Who knows, one day, I'll get so hot, I'll explode in the middle of the night.

7   A spiked drink (Godwilling's talk)

—I miss my home, back in Italy.
—I'd like a little place of my own too, where I could
return to and feel cosy.
—Don't you have one, Anna?
—I haven't got one. None of us women have one.
—How come?
—You men come back home. We are the home.
(Extract from a dialogue between the Italian
and Godwilling)

Massimo Risi arrived at the headquarters of the administration in a sweat. Before going in, he sniffed himself and frowned: he could still smell Temporina's perfume. He asked me whether it was noticeable and I set his mind at rest, hurrying him along to the office. He still had the strong taste in his mouth of the drink Temporina had given him. He swallowed various times. He was late, but the minister made no mention of time. Satisfied, he pointed to the tape recorder:

—*I've spoken to Anna Godwilling. I've recorded everything, as we agreed.*

I looked around in surprise: the minister was alone. Neither the administrator nor Chupanga were in the room. We sat down while the representative of the government pressed the button on the tape recorder and the prostitute's voice spread to every corner of the room. The Italian couldn't disguise a quiver. Godwilling's voice was carnal, inflaming, like some drink that banishes one's power of reason. The two men gazed beyond the confines of the walls, with an absent look in their eye. They remained like that, bedazzled, for some time. Massimo buried his head in his hands and asked the minister to start the tape again from the beginning. Once again, Godwilling's words filled the place:

Let me begin by explaining my work. But first I want to say this: sometime soon, you will stop being a minister. You'll cross over and become an ex-minister. But I'll never cross over to become anything else. A whore is never an ex-one. There are ex-nurses, ex-ministers, but there aren't any ex-prostitutes. Whoring is a life sentence, a stain you can never wash off.

Let me explain, don't interrupt me. You, sir, are a minister, I'm just a simple between-the-sheets woman. You'll hear more tittle-tattle out there than you will leaves being trodden on. I've been a woman of ill-repute for a long time now. But all their talk amounts to nothing but malicious barbs. People gossip that I give my body away, I do it for free when they can't pay. They say I indulge in hanky-panky to order, just like that, for the souls of the dead. Is it worth answering such lies?

It's as useless as cleaning the rust from a nail. I know what I do in life. The one who knows the dirt on the wall is the snail that climbs up it. No one else.

Do you know what I think now? I'm going around opening my thighs to the ungrateful, and it's like scratching a stone with one's nails. This world has got more teeth in it than mouths. It's easier to bite than it is to kiss, believe me, sir. I'm taking the opportunity to say all this because I've never spoken to a minister from the government before, do you understand?

The minister stopped the recorder. He looked at the Italian, who had a blank expression on his face. The foreigner only emerged from his immobility to smell himself.

—*Do you want me to wind it forward a bit?*

—*No, let it play*— Massimo replied.

—*It's just that there are one or two passages here* ...

—*Let the tape play.*

—*I don't think it's going to shed any more light.*

—*Do you know what's at stake in this whole matter?*

—*But it's never going to be resolved, you people don't understand* ...

—*Minister, you know only too well that this has got to be cleared up.*

The minister seemed to have resigned himself, when there was a knock on the door. It was the adjutant, Chupanga. The minister didn't allow him to come in. He didn't want anyone else witnessing those confessions. Once again, he pressed the 'play' button. The voice of Anna Godwilling filled the large room once more.

Sit down here, Your Excellency. Sit down, the mattress is

clean and the sheet has just been washed. That's it, right there. I couldn't see you properly where you were before. You've got famished eyes, sir. Begging your pardon, but it's through people's eyes that I see most things. Everyday routines, fame and glory, the thirst for beyond: everything's written in a person's look. Do you want to lean back on this cushion? No? That's all right. You make yourself at home as you wish, sir.

Right. Now I'll get back to the matter in hand. Do you want to know the whole truth about what happened? Yes indeed, sir, the foreign soldiers are exploding. But it's not because they're stepping on mines. It's we women who are their combustion. Don't look at me like that. We have powers, you know. Or have you forgotten the strength of the earth? Ask around, everyone knows. The people don't talk, but gossip is always being born. Grass produces flowers, even though it doesn't seem to. Only those far away can't see. We only pretend to remain silent. You know that, don't you, sir? You can put your arm on my upper leg, there's no problem. Come on, don't stay over there all shy and coy, you're like an anteater.

I'm going to tell you what happens, and I'll tell you what happened that night. But first, let me undo a couple of buttons. See how you're sweating, sir.

The minister's zealous finger once again pressed the 'stop' button. He took a deep breath and knocked back a whole glass of water.

—*Have some, it's been boiled.*

The Italian drank two glasses. He seemed to have faith in that water, with its title, source and guarantee on the bottle. He needed to wash himself inside. And he was beginning to be suspicious of the drink Temporina had made him the previous evening.

—*You see what people are like round here? They talk a lot but don't say much. This woman hasn't said anything yet.*

—*But I need concrete information. People don't just disappear.*

—*They exploded. You don't believe it, but that's what really happened*— the minister insisted, trying to open a warped window.

—*But how? Exploded without any explosives?*

—*That's what the prostitute told me.*

—*Switch the recorder on. I want to hear it right through to the end.*

—*No, it's better if I sum it up for you. We're using up the batteries.*

—*I'll send for some more.*

Against his will, the minister switched on Anna Godwilling's statement. And once again, her rich warm voice spread like rain falling in our soul.

The Zambian soldier arrived, showing off his uniform. He walked into the bar, belching his presence. He clicked his heels and ordered drink. We didn't like those superior airs, you know. We just pretended to be pleasant, that was all. I noticed someone put some special powder, one of our spells, in his drink. I didn't know who or what it was. The work of men, the jealousy of those who didn't want their womenfolk interfered with. As for me, Excellency, I actually feel proud of their jealousy. For I've never belonged to anyone. Never. If there were men fighting over me, I felt I belonged, as if I belonged exclusively to one man. But that's how it was. What I'm telling you has neither ears nor mouth. I saw those powders falling like sand into the wretched man's beer. I saw everything. When that Zambian took me by the hand, I already knew what fate had in store for him. I went off with him without any feeling of pity ...

Yet again, the recording was stopped. The Italian asked testily:

—*Does it end just like that? It looks as if it's been cut.*

—*Cut? Who?*

—*Yes, the woman seemed to want to go on talking.*

—*Ah! But she was just talking about ... she was talking the local language.*

—*And what was she saying?*

—*It's just that I can't understand this folk's dialect very well.*

He gathered up some papers and put them in his case, explaining that he had some urgent matters to deal with in the capital. He couldn't prolong his stay in such an out-of-the-way place. He was leaving that very afternoon. He had left clear instructions with the local administration.

—*You stay and speak to whoever you want and think fit. I've left orders for you to be given free access to everything and everyone.*

Then the minister asked me to go to the secretary's office and call for the adjutant, Chupanga. I went out into the building, aware that I had been asked to leave so that the government representative and Risi could talk confidentially. It was already late afternoon, and the office staff had already knocked off work. Only the faithful

Chupanga remained. He was greatly surprised when I called him. Was envy gnawing away at him because I had been accepted into the intimacy of our superiors in their conversations? For the first time, the man who appeared before me looked submissive and awkward. And then he was quick to suggest the reason.

—*I know, it must be because of His Excellency's photograph.*

And he walked towards the office to which he had been summoned with a huge frame in his hand. As he went in, the first question the minister asked was:

—*Haven't you hung the frame up yet?*

Chupanga was quick to express his apologies. It was a presidential portrait and the walls needed to be thoroughly cleaned before the official frame was put up.

—*Say hello to Senhor Risi here. He's going to be working with you on this matter.*

The adjutant Chupanga got all mixed up as to which hand he should shake. Meanwhile, he lost his grip on the picture, which fell to the ground, smashing its glass. The man quivered, terrified by the minister's stern look:

—*My God!*

And he stepped back as if he feared the splinters would jump up at him. And now? What now? The minister was asking him. There wouldn't be any sheets of glass in town. How was he going to cover the photograph, protect His Excellency from the solar and non-solar rays? Chupanga was unable to stitch words together. Suddenly, he dashed off down the corridor and soon returned with another sheet of glass.

—See, Your Excellency, I've found another glass. I took it off the previous portrait ...

He didn't finish his sentence. There was the sound of an almighty explosion: the world seemed to be coming apart. Whole windows were smashed and the Italian was hurled back against the wall. I too was knocked right into the middle of the floor. Having recovered from the fright, I saw Chupanga, forlornly holding a chink of glass, while the administrator was rushing outside, puffing and panting. We ran after him. Outside, folk seemed to have parted company with order. There was complete chaos. The minister ordered us to go back inside. There was no point in taking any risks. He would send some people out to discover what had happened. In the meantime, we should return to the guesthouse to await further instructions.

At the guesthouse, they gave us the news: there had been another of those strange explosions not far from there. It was another United Nations soldier who had dissolved mysteriously just a short distance from where they were.

—This time, they say it was a Pakistani.

Only later would we find out what had happened through a report from the local administrator. The minister had insisted he file one right away. The following morning, I was summoned and handed an envelope. I was told to communicate its contents informally to the Italian, for the papers didn't bear an official seal. They had been written in the form of a letter, sincere in hand and in heart. It went on to reveal details of the explosion: the latest victim was a Pakistani, responsible for guarding the official residence of the administrator, Estêvão Jonas. This time, the explosion had occurred right at the centre of power.

When I got to my room, all alone and by myself, I began to read Estêvão Jonas's typescript. What I found strange was the human tone of his letter. I made a point of reading outside the lines.

8 The phallic fan

> *The monkey went mad*
> *from trying to see what lay behind the mirror.*
> (Proverb)

His Excellency
The Minister Responsible

I am writing this helter-skelter: what I saw made me blind; it was what I didn't see that made things clear. When I heard that flash blowing a hole through the sunset, I was suspicious: could it be a lure? Inviting me to place my feet on the road to danger? The enemy is everywhere, even in our underwear. This is the background to my report on the latest incident. Which was a real storm that spilled over the teacup.

Do you remember, Excellency, that I asked for leave yesterday afternoon? I was getting some papers together at home, some documents for Your Excellency to take back with you to the capital. It so happens that at that very hour a certain lady – whose name I cannot mention – was preparing me a whisky out of a black-labelled bottle. Excellency, it's just that I'm unable to refuel with just any woman or any beverage. I'm a cultured man, and whisky is an old and cherished friend of mine.

Well, Excellency, I was just beginning my intimacies with the anonymous female. I won't go into details, but let me just confide this terror I have of my hands catching fire. It happens with Ermelinda: hardly have I embarked on my foreplay than my fingers burst into heat. But with this other nameless woman – the curse threatened to get out of control. So there was I, that afternoon, rubbing against her, without managing to dispel my fear of burning. As a precaution, I made sure I cooled the tips of my fingers on the ice cubes in my whisky. I was getting to the stage of lying on top of her when there was a blinding flash and it was as if the universe was being torn in two. I got such a fright that I felt myself at that very instant to check my affliction – was it I who had exploded? And I looked up at the heavens, appealing for mercy to the powers over life.

That was when I saw flying through the air towards me, more swiftly than a lightning flash, a male organ. My eyes popped out like marbles. Even now I can't stop stammering: my tongue keeps seeking my gullet whenever I try to describe what happened. Fortunately, the lady in question beat a hasty retreat. At first, I thought she might have been pulverised by the explosion. But no, through a slit in the shutters I saw her running for dear life down the street.

You can accuse me, sir. I have a back as wide as a turtle's. But I'm describing things exactly as they occurred. Well, the flying sex organ, after brushing against my person, went and lodged itself on the blade of the ceiling fan. And round and round it went up there, like a tightrope walker high up in the circus tent.

I decided to increase the speed of the fan. Maybe the object would come unstuck in centrifugal weakness. I turned it up to maximum speed. But nothing happened: the dangling thing refused to dislodge itself, suspended there, convinced it was still alive. Was it playing hard to get?

Let me explain the background to the incident: I had ordered some young goats to be slaughtered for Your Excellency to take back to the capital. Apparently, goats are no longer allowed to board planes. But when it comes to people in government, exceptions can always be made, isn't that so? Life isn't just a string of sacrifices. Well, that afternoon, I had so many adjutants killing so many goats out in the back yard. When the explosion occurred, everyone ran for cover. Total confusion set in, with the goats bounding off down the road, and folk derailing left right and centre. After some time, those same people crowded together near the henhouse. Up there, on the wooden planks, lay the unfortunate fellow's boots. But there was no other sign of him: no blood, no gore, not even a whiff. The great unasked question hung in the air: where had that whoremonger of a Pakistani ended up?

When my wife arrived, I had to lie. I couldn't reveal who I was with when the incident occurred. But the glasses of whisky incriminated me. Dona Ermelinda, my spouse, got straight to the point:

—There are two glasses here.

—Yes, I was having a drink with Major Ahmed.

—Who is Ahmed?

—Was. He was the man who got blown away. The Head of Security.

—And this Head of Security, this major, did he use lipstick?

I muttered a how should I know. Who knows what the habits of these Asians are? Don't some of them go around wearing skirts? Who knows what they wear inside their clothes. And I pointed to the ceiling. It was better that she should see the soldier's organ so as to banish any suspicions. It was only afterwards that I felt embarrassment at having to confess that the male instrument was skewered, head downwards, so to speak, on the ceiling of my house. I was deceiving Ermelinda. But the others, what would they think? That I was involved in the famous explosions? Or worse, that I was fooling around with men, and brown ones at that?

At first, Ermelinda seemed puzzled. Then she pursued her doubts with renewed vigour, running her fingers round the marks on the ill-fated glass.

—So it was the major, was it?

—What do you want me to do about it, dear wife? These are cultural matters.

—And getting it up the arse, is that a cultural matter?

I couldn't allow such language. But for the moment, there was some advantage to be gained from all the confusion. That was when the other blue helmets came in, together with our soldiers. They rummaged around here and there: what were they looking for? Exactly, the Pakistani's attachment. My wife, with a sardonic laugh, exclaimed:

—Ah! Is that what you're looking for? Well, ask the administrator here.

By this time I was weak at the knees as I pointed up at the ceiling. At that point, I was overcome by giddiness and I collapsed on the floor. They helped me up, all drooping, limp and unconscious. I remained in a faint for some time. When I came round, I felt myself all over. I wanted to make sure I was intact and all there. Then I smiled, relieved: once again I'd even believed myself to be in the realm of the exploded, my soul ground to husk, my body to dust. And it's from the same bed where they placed me that I am writing these contorted lines to you. I beg your patience for these confessions.

Now then: the situation isn't quite like that about which I wrote in the report that was handed to you by the ex-comrade minister. It's far more serious. It's this problem of the exploding men. I have even wondered whether it's not some spell ordered because of my stepson Jonassane. You know that he's involved with dubious characters who steal and even dabble in drug dealing. I'm worried, so much so that I even gave him an ambulance sent us by some project in support of our health service. I diverted the vehicle for the lad to get involved in the transport business. It kept him occupied and he always made a bit of money. But then things became complicated for me, what with all these accusations of corruption and counter-corruption, and I ended up returning the ambulance. I'm now asking some South Africans who want to settle here to give me a new vehicle. They give me one, and I make things easier for them. Is that wrong? Ermelinda doesn't think so at all: he who doesn't weep, doesn't eat. When it comes down to it, how do we make ends meet? Are we supposed to summon morality into our lives when morality doesn't want anything at all to do with us? Anyway, these are the thoughts I have brought home with me, my privatised preoccupations. I hope you will give me the benefit of your pardon.

At present, all that you hear in the district are stories, tittle-tattle. The people talk without any constraint, mumbling and jumbling about the explosions. And they say the land is going to burn because of the government leaders who don't respect traditions and don't observe ceremonies in honour of their ancestors. That's how they talk, citing and reciting. What can I do? They're black, of course, like me. But they're not of my race. I'm sorry, Excellency, it's possible I may be an ethnic racist. I admit it. But these folk don't chime with me. Sometimes they oppress me because I feel ashamed of them. It's hard working with the proletariat. I don't even know what to call them anymore: the proletariat, the people, the population, the local communities. One big headache, these poor folk, if it weren't for them, our task would be easier.

My wife, the ex-comrade Ermelinda, doesn't help me either. She loves the power and the wealth, but she is the recipient of bad influences. Sometimes she frequents the very un-Catholic mass of that priest, Father Muhando. I even suspect she visits the witchdoctor, the so-called Zeca Andorinho. And afterwards, as a result, Ermelinda gets irritated with me to the point where we argue in public. She even called me an obstinate old devil. Just imagine. And what's more, she said that Father Muhando was right after all: Hell doesn't have enough room for so many demons. We're getting the surplus here on Earth. What you might call exiles from Hell, if you see what I mean. And we, the old revolutionaries, form part of this surplus. Those are Muhando's words, I'm sure. We were socialist tricksters and now we're tricked capitalists. And if we once had doubts, now we have debts. They are her words, the aforementioned Ermelinda, who takes advantage of any topic to give herself a longer tongue.

You know only too well, sir: an administrator's work doesn't earn a wage you can dig your fingers into. Fortunately, things have changed, we're opening our eyes and making up for the lean years. I've now got my properties, and my business ventures are beginning to look up. I've already embarked on partnerships with the South Africans who've turned up here. I've given them some land, all on the basis of you scratch my back and I'll scratch yours. But this isn't to be talked about, for the moment people start exhibiting their wealth, jealousy isn't far behind.

I am writing these things, Comrade Excellency, because we are politically compromised. As they say: neighbours' houses burn together. I am troubled, Honourable Comrade, by the following doubt: could it be that Father Muhando is right? Should we perhaps not be taking greater care of the life of the masses? For the truth is that the snail never throws away its shell. The people are the shell that protects us. But it could, all of a sudden, turn into the fire that will consume us. It even causes me to shiver just to think about it, I who have felt my hands burning. This, Excellency, is a struggle between life and death and vice versa.

I shall sign off by sending you my most sincere revolutionary greetings. Or more properly: I remain most fiducially yours.

Estêvão Jonas
District Administrator

9 The swoon

> *Does a dog lick its wounds?*
> *Or is it death, by means of an open sore,*
> *that kisses the puppy on the mouth?*
> (Saying from Tizangara)

—*Don't look now*— I said.

—*What is it?*— asked Massimo, alarmed.

It wasn't anything important, just the man who had turned up some days before, the owner of the ill-fated goat. We weren't quick enough to avoid him. The fellow accosted us, full of whimpers:

—*Well then, bosses?*

This time I pointed to the Italian. It was he who should listen to all the whining. I had been forewarned: if you give alms to a beggar, even the largest amount possible, he will always walk off empty-handed. But this man wasn't presenting himself as a beggar. He was seeking compensation for a loss: it wasn't just any old billy-goat, it was a mating animal, that only left him to go and cover so many nanny-goats. For the rest of the time, it was just like a dog, even barking at cats. And when it came to wagging his tail, he did it more elegantly even than Anna Godwilling.

—*It would be better to give him something*— I suggested to Massimo.

After all, the poor fellow had enough misfortune to contend with. He was a shepherd who worked for Estêvão Jonas. But he hadn't been paid for months. I didn't want to have to listen to the long litany of complaints. If Massimo wouldn't give anything, I was even prepared to bail the poor man out. But the UN delegate felt in his pockets and took out a dollar note. He held it out to the plaintiff, who examined the note with great care and shook his head: the money was spoiled. Let God forgive him for cursing the sacred scrap of paper, but he would prefer the local notes, greasy though they were. Besides, because of the trauma felt at seeing his beloved goat die at his feet, he had begun to feel itches all over his body. He was therefore in need of medical care, who knows, maybe for the rest of his life. And that was an illness requiring more than just a mere banknote.

The Italian, fed up, turned his back and walked towards the administration building. The aggrieved goatherd stood there, contemplating the dollar for all to see. I ran to catch up with Massimo, who was already peering through the window of the old building. It was now confirmed: the radio transmitter had been fully installed in the headquarters of the administration, in a room that only he had access to. I had helped him to put in the machinery and erect the antenna. We had tested it and everything worked.

But the Italian was still not happy. And he was right: the following day, the radio transmitter was no longer there. It had disappeared in strange circumstances.

Now, with his blue beret in his hand, Massimo was consumed by consummate anxiety: another soldier reduced to a sexual organ! What could he write in his report? That his men were exploding like soap bubbles? In the capital, the UN mission headquarters expected concrete news and plausible explanations. And what had he managed to clarify? Half a dozen hysterical stories, as far as he was concerned. He felt all alone, with the weight of Africa upon him.

—*What a dog's life!*— he mused, with a sigh.

The sigh gave him no relief. For a fear was added to his dejection: what if he really had made love to Temporina? His memories were so vivid and flavoursome that he took it as fact.

—*So, why are you scared then?*— I asked.

—*Don't you understand? If I did, I did it without any protection!*

—*What do you fear most: that you've caught an illness or that you've caught the curse of the exploding men?*

I tried to make a joke of it to lighten the moment. But Risi didn't laugh. What I thought of as a joke now became a motive for a greater sense of incumbency. Hadn't he taken a risk? Who knows whether he wouldn't be blown to smithereens one day like some former blue helmet?

—*I didn't think of that.*

—*When it comes down to it, do you believe in the spell?*

—*I don't know what the hell I believe in.*

—*The spell's probably reserved for military personnel, relax, Massimo Risi.*

In order to disperse the dark clouds, I suggested we go for a walk, unmapped and with no particular destination. The minister had already gone, having left instructions on how work should continue. Massimo Risi was now head of the investigation, sole representative of the world in our little town.

We strolled casually past crowded street corners, where hawkers gathered. The receptionist from the guesthouse emerged from the crowd. He looked worried. He'd been sent by Temporina to look for her simpleton brother.

—*We haven't seen him*— Massimo informed him.

The hotelier called me aside and mumbled cautiously:

—*That white guy mustn't hear what I've got to say.*

—*So what is it?*

—*It's that the lad left the house saying he was going to kill someone.*

—*Who was he going to kill?*

—*The Italian.*

Kill Massimo? Why? Jealousy maybe. Fear that the European might take his sister far away. What couldn't be doubted was that the boy was wandering around the side streets of Tizangara in a demented state, and might even have set off into the bush. Temporina was concerned: the boy had no experience of travelling the roads of the world.

I reassured the receptionist. If I saw the boy, I would accompany him back to Hortensia's house, his maternal home.

—*My home too*— added the receptionist timidly —*I'm a*

distant brother of Hortensia.

—*Are you Temporina's uncle?*

—*Keep it to yourself.*

Such talk was pretence. In Tizangara, who wasn't a distant brother? But I accepted it. The man was explaining why Temporina had become attached to the guesthouse. She was among family. No one was a prisoner except of their own destiny.

Oblivious to all this, Massimo Risi shook invisible dust from his jacket. As he was doing this, the buttons fell off. How come? Clearly, they must have already been loose. He laughed as he recalled the letters that had fallen off the front of the guesthouse. He knelt down to pick up the buttons. However, as he was trying to gather them, he noticed his fingers warping and growing stiff. The more he tried, the less success he had. He decided to get up and get out of there. I couldn't understand what was happening inside him, the man didn't utter a word. At first, he thought it might be the result of the drink. What the hell had he been given to drink? But then, to his horror, he found that he couldn't even get up. He couldn't even change position. He looked up, and that was when he saw the old-young girl from the guesthouse. She was a sight to be disbelieved, nor did she resemble any human form. Massimo blurted:

—*Temporina?*

The woman caressed his head. This was the vision he later told me he had had. But the girl was not behaving sweetly. She pulled his head back and kissed him as if she were sucking his soul out with her lips. Then, she grabbed the Italian's hand and guided it to her belly, as if she were teaching him to recognise a part of her anatomy that had always belonged to him.

—*Massimo Risi?*

Chupanga's voice awoke him as if it were coming from another world.

—*There you are lying on the ground ... Don't tell me you fainted?!*

The administrator's adjutant had arrived at that very moment and had been struck by what he saw. We helped him up. The European took a few steps back, and another few forward. Maybe he was looking for himself. And rightly so. After all, he had almost forborne himself, and hadn't recovered from the fright. He looked up at the sky, but then immediately withdrew his gaze: the light there was too clean. Chupanga, all unctuous, made to lead him to some shade.

—*You know, I've been wanting to have a talk with you, a very private one so to speak.*

The Italian was still in a daze. There, unhelped by distance, he was a very vulnerable soul. He said he would prefer to go back to the guesthouse, but Chupanga was insistent:

—*Ever since you arrived, I've been looking for a chance to talk to you but ... a bit to one side, if you see what I mean.*

He glanced at me out of the corner of his eye. He suggested I should make myself scarce. But Massimo rejected the idea. He wanted me to stay near him. So as to translate, he commented ironically. Chupanga had a ball of wool in his throat, and he found it difficult to unravel his speech:

—*It's that I know many things. But for a man to talk, he needs fuel.*

—*Fuel?*

Chupanga looked at me, this time imploring complicity. I stood there impassively, as if I myself didn't understand him. So he returned to the fray, circling the Italian:

—*Think about it. I know some very valuable things. But we need to talk like men who understand each other, are you with me?*

—*I'll think about the matter*— said the foreigner abruptly.

—*But please don't mention it to anyone*— and turning to me he added brusquely —*make sure you don't talk to that fellow of yours ...*

—*Who?*

—*Your father, old Sulplício.*

I knew it: my father dwelt far from the favour of those in government. But the people held him in respect, because of the collection of ancestors he could call upon from eternity. In the words of Chupanga, my father belonged to the nation of beasts, he was as difficult as a threadworm, all artful and insinuating. The first time he had tried to speak to him, the administrator had felt the weight of ridicule. There he was, all style and manners, if you please here, excuse me there. And the other fellow, not a word, his brow bolted, licking his own tongue. That is: not speaking Portuguese, but the local language. Old Sulplício didn't respect any presence. Until they decided to teach him a lesson.

The Italian got up, for he wanted to return to the guesthouse on foot. But the representative of bureaucracy insisted. They would go by car, which was safer. Besides, no one respects you if you don't arrive envehicled. Chupanga pointed ostentatiously to a car.

—*It's a turbo-diesel with a good few horse power. It's got air-conditioning throughout.*

We got into the car. Chupanga turned on the air-conditioning and opened a can of beer. He offered us a drink. Only I accepted. On the way, the Italian broke the silence:

—*I'm worried about this situation.*

—*Me too*— said Chupanga. —*But I've already ordered a brand-new frame from the capital.*

When we reached the guesthouse, the Italian got out of the car without saying goodbye. I followed him and noticed that he was walking in a more sprightly fashion, that he was moving as if his body belonged to him. We both sat down in the bar. We talked, for no other reason than to pass the time. After a while, I said:

—*You know, Massimo, I pity you being all alone. I couldn't bear to be left so utterly on my own.*

—*Why?*

—*Even if I was torn away from here, if I was taken to Italy, I wouldn't be in such a difficult position. Because I know how to live in your world.*

—*And I don't know how to live in yours?*

—*No, you don't.*

—*That doesn't bother me. All I want is to carry out my mission. You don't know how important this is for me, for my career. And for Mozambique.*

He tried to explain himself: my security depended on others, his lay in his career. I felt sorry for him. For he was searching like a blind man. He wasn't taking due care: truth has long legs and treads the path of deceit. To make matters worse, in Tizangara, everything happened in a hurry. Those who came here never came to stay. That's why when those soldiers arrived from the United Nations, they were called grasshoppers.

—*Another thing: you ask too many questions. Truth escapes many questions.*

—*How can I get answers if I don't ask questions?*

—*Do you know what you should do? You should tell your story. We are waiting for you whites to tell us your stories.*

—*A story? I don't know any stories.*

—*You do, you must know. Even the dead know. They tell stories through the mouths of the living.*

—*While we're on the subject, I've been going round asking other people. But I haven't yet asked you: were you here when the explosions began?*

—*Yes, I was.*

—*Then you've seen it all. Tell me. Tell me everything, ever since the first bang. One moment. Wait: I want to record you. I hope you don't mind.*

10 *The first bursts*

Facts are only true
after they've been invented
(A belief from Tizangara)

The first time I heard the explosions, I thought the war had returned, bringing with it all its troops and troubles. I only had one thought in my mind: to get away. I passed the last houses of Tizangara, my tiny home town. In the distance, I could still see the silhouette of the house where I had been born, and then, somewhat nearer, Dona Hortensia's residence and the church tower. The town seemed to be taking its leave of the world, as sad as a tortoise crossing the desert.

I ran away to the bush, there where no one had ever become a person. Yes, it was true: that forest had never before welcomed any human being. I built a shelter from leaves and branches. Not much, and indistinguishable from that of an animal: it wouldn't be good for someone to be seen there in the form of a person. I had a shelter, not an address. I remained in my hiding-place, counselled by my fear. I would go back to the town when I was certain the war hadn't returned. But on the very first night, the noise of the animals and even more so the shadows of darkness, filled me with alarm. I trembled with fear: had I not jumped from the hyena's mouth into the lion's throat?

I sat down to gather my thoughts. My soul seemed to have left me and was hovering like a cloud above me. The war had ended almost a year before. We hadn't understood the war, and now we didn't understand the peace. But everything seemed to be going well, after the guns had fallen silent. But as far as the elders were concerned, everything had been decided: the ancestors had sat down, dead and alive, and had awoken a time propitious for peace. If the chiefs, during this new time, respected the harmony between the earth and the spirits, then good rains would fall and men would harvest general happiness. Full of precaution, I had my doubts about this. The new chiefs seemed to care little for the fortune of others. I was talking of what I saw there in Tizangara. I had nothing to say about anywhere else. But in my town, there was now as much injustice as in colonial times. It was as if, in another way, that time had not ended. What was happening was that it was being administered by people of another race.

Perhaps it was, after all, some great fatigue that caused me to remain out there, far away. Secretly, I had fallen out of love with that town. Or it was probably not the town, but the life I led there. I no longer had sufficient faith to turn my country into a well-shaded place. This was the fault of

the current regime of our existence. Those who governed us
in Tizangara grew visibly more prosperous in girth, they
stole land from the peasants, grew drunk without respect
for anyone. Envy was the greatest commandment. But the
land is a being: it lacks a family, that weave of
interdependent existences we call tenderness. The newly
rich went around pillaging the territory, they had no
country. Without any love for the living or respect for the
dead. I missed the others that they had once been. For
when it came to it, they were rich but had no wealth at all.
They deceived themselves by having cars, and one or two
easily exhausted baubles. They spoke ill of foreigners by
day. By night, they knelt at their feet, exchanging favours
for crumbs. They wanted to command without governing.
They wanted to grow rich without working.

Now, in the isolation of the forest, I watched time pass
by without anything ever happening. That was what gave
me pleasure: to think without ever having an idea. Was I,
after all, turning into an animal, into the logic of claws and
talons? What had the war done to us? The strange thing
was that in fifteen years of shooting, I had not been killed,
only to succumb when peace was secure. I hadn't died of
the illness, so was I now dying of the cure?

It was on one morning during this retreat that I became
aware of voices. They made themselves heard in
camouflage. I followed the sounds with the greatest
precaution. These were people who thought no one could
see them. I peered through the thickets. I glimpsed some
shapes. There were both blacks and whites. They were
bending over the ground and it looked as if they were

digging by the side of a path. After a while, one of them spoke in a loud clear voice. There was a shout in a foreigner's English:

—*Attention!*

The others stopped. Then they retreated unhurriedly. From time to time, they bent down again in a circle round some other object. What were they looking for? But then they went away and I was left alone once more. I gave them time to get some distance away before going over to see what it was they had been excavating. That was when an arm stopped me.

—*Don't go any further. It's dangerous!*

I turned: it was my mother. Or maybe it was a vision I had of her. For she had long ago crossed the frontier of life to the great beyond. But at that moment, she emerged from the foliage, wrapped in her usual dark cloth: she didn't greet me, but merely guided me back to my shelter. There she sat down, huddled in her *capulana*. I waited like a quiet child. If we have a voice, it is to pour out our feelings. On the other hand, an excess of feeling robs us of our voice. Now that she had crossed from one state to another, she could see me quite clearly.

—*What's this, son: are you living where animals live?*

I returned her question with another:

—*Is there anywhere nowadays that isn't the realm of animals?*

She smiled sadly. She could have answered: yes, there is, where I come from is where people live. But she remained silent. She walked round the bushes and crushed leaves between her fingers. She was concocting perfumes and lifting them slowly to her face. She was having a taste of bygone smells.

—*Has the war come back, mother?*

—*The war never left, son. Wars are like the seasons of the year: they remain in suspense, ripening in the hatred of the narrow-minded.*

—*And what are you doing round here, mother?*

I wanted to know whether she had finished her task of dying. She explained herself slowly and at length. She was going around with a pot to collect the tears of all the mothers in the world. She wanted to make one whole sea out of them. Don't smile at me like that, you don't know how important the business of crying is. What does a tear do? A tear puts us in touch with the universe, in a tear we return to our origins. That little drop in us is the navel of the world. A tear plagiarises the ocean. She was thinking by using other, non-existent words. And she sighed:

—*Dear God!*

She reminded me of how she used to wake up soaking wet. After my father left us, not a morning went by when the sun found her in dry clothes. She was forever in tears. But this had been before, when she was suffering from the illness of being alive.

—*Don't stay here, for war still stalks these parts. Its footprint is alive!*

—*I feel so well here, mother. I don't feel like going back.*

We sat there for hours swapping pleasantries, and merely passing the time. Making the miracle of our being there on the edge of the forest linger a while longer. By now, it was beginning to get late, and she advised me:

—*Go back to the town, so many things are going to happen.*

—*Before you go, mother, remind me about the story of the flamingo.*

—*Ah! It's such an old story …*

—*Tell it to me, mother. It's for the journey. I feel such a need for a journey.*

—*Then sit down, my son. I'll tell it to you. But promise me one thing first: never follow in the tracks of those men you were watching a little while ago.*

—*I promise.*

Then she murmured the story to me. I repeated it word for word, copying her tired voice. She recounted: there was a place where time hadn't invented night. It was always day. Until the flamingo said:

—*Today, I shall make my last flight!*

The other birds, taken unawares, were devastated. But in spite of their sadness, they didn't cry. A bird's sadness hasn't invented tears. People say: the tears of birds are kept up there where the rain never falls.

At the flamingo's warning, all the birds gathered together. There would be an assembly to discuss the matter. While they were waiting for the flamingo, the sound of chirping could be heard hovering in the air. Were such words credible? They might be, or then again they might not. Whatever the case, they all asked themselves:

—*But where is he going to fly to?*

—*To some spot where there's no place.*

The long-legged creature arrived at last, and explained – that there were two skies, one facing this way, and possible to fly in, and the other, the sky with all the stars, and inappropriate for flight. He wanted to cross that frontier.

—*Why such a journey devoid of return?*

The flamingo made little of his intended act:

—*Ah! Although it's far, it's not distant.*

Then, he went in among the shady trees of the mangrove. There he lingered. He only reappeared when the patience of the others was ageing fast. The winged creatures gathered in the marshland clearing. And they all gazed at the flamingo as if, only then, they were becoming aware of all his beauty. He advanced proudly, haughtily controlling his height. The others stood in a line to bid him farewell. One of them tried to make him go back on his word.

—*Please don't go!*

—*I must go!*

The ostrich intervened and told him:

—*Look at me: I who have never flown carry my wings like two distant yearnings. And yet my steps have only encountered happiness.*

—*I can't. I've grown tired of living in one body.*

And he had spoken. He wanted to go where there was no shade nor map. Where everything is light while never becoming day. In that other world he would sleep, sleep like a desert, forget that he could fly, turn his back on the art of landing on the earth's surface.

—*I don't want to come to land anymore. I just want to come to rest.*

And he gazed upwards. The sky looked low, unassuming. But its blue was so intense that it was reflected in the eyes of the animals.

Then the flamingo launched himself, bow and arrow stiffened in his body. And off he flew like the chosen one, elegant, shedding his weight. Seen in flight like that, it was as if the sky had gained a vertebra and the cloud, out there ahead, was merely the soul of a bird. One could say even more: that it was light itself that was in flight. And with each flap of its wings, the bird was slowly turning the sky's transparent pages. One more beat of its feathers and suddenly it looked to everyone as if the horizon were growing red. It turned from blue to darker tones, reds and mauves. Everything changing as if ablaze. Thus was the first sunset born. When the flamingo was lost from sight, night descended upon the earth for the first time.

That was the end of the story. In the darkness, my mother's voice faded away. I looked at the sunset and saw the birds carrying the sun, pushing the day to elsewhere and beyond.

That was my last night in the bushland hideout. The next morning, I returned to town, like someone returning to his own body after sleep.

11   *The first culprit*

> *A nation's ruins*
> *begin in its humble citizen's home.*
> (African proverb)

The following day, I was summoned by the administrator. The message was clear: I was to turn up without the Italian. At the entrance to the building, Chupanga received me with his usual arrogance. Without looking at me, he pointed to a chair. I was told to wait. A group of white people came into the waiting room. The adjutant got up, all subservient, exceeding himself in pleasantries and gestures.

—*Who are they?*— I asked Chupanga.

—*They're from the mine clearance programme.*

—*Are they still clearing mines?*

—*The people from the NGOs are going around saying all the mines have been cleared. It's a lie. There's still lots of work to be done.*

—*And where are these mines?*

—*That's what we don't know. We only know there are some because they keep appearing.*

I remembered what I had seen when I fled to the bush: the strange group of people rummaging around in the undergrowth. I thought I recognised one of those who was coming out. I was still probing Chupanga for explanations, when a voice ordered me to step forward. It would be better if I kept my thoughts to myself. Finally, the secretary ushered me in. His Excellency was ready to receive me.

—*When I arranged for you to be my translator, you didn't understand the deal*— said Estêvão Jonas the moment I sat down.

—*I'm sorry, but I don't understand.*

—*You see? You still don't understand. You don't understand what I expect of you.*

—*And what is that, Excellency?*

—*To keep an eye on that white bastard. That Italian who's going round sticking his nose in other people's business.*

—*But I thought he was here to help us.*

—*Help?! Don't you realise? No one helps anyone nowadays in this world. Don't you know the saying: a bat casts its shadow on the ceiling?*

Then the administrator confessed: he'd got Chupanga to spy on me. His plan was threefold espionage: I would spy on the Italian, Chupanga would spy on me, and last but not least, he would spy on all of us.

—*To be honest, I have my doubts about you. It's because of your father.*

—*I've got nothing to do with him, Excellency.*

—*No? I don't know, I just don't know. You're father and son, and a beard always lies up against a head of hair.*

And apart from that, he stressed, why had my old man turned up in town at this precise moment? He couldn't understand this sudden return.

—*Yes indeed, what are the reasons for this? And it's not so much a question of his reasons, but his motives.*

When I left, he gave me a warning: I should be sensible. What was at play was not a simple matter. He knew only too well what he was talking about. He looked at me with complacency:

—*The first time I passed through here, you weren't even born. You remind me of my late wife. Ah! That woman ...*

It sent a shiver through me. Estêvão Jonas was recalling my mother with such raptures? He read the doubts in my thoughts. And he recalled:

—*I arrived here while I was still a guerrilla fighter.*

—*So I've been told.*

—*Don't forget that, ever: I'm the one who freed the fatherland! I'm the one who freed you, my young friend.*

A slight twitch of his finger was his signal for me to leave. Once in the street, I was surprised by the clamour of the people. I could hear voices:

—*They've caught him! They've caught the exploder!*

A hubbub of folk gathered in the street. Among them, I had a clear view of the Italian. It was obvious that he had come out in a hurry, for he was still buttoning himself up and tidying his hair. I joined him.

—*What's happening?*

—*A man's been arrested.*

We approached the policemen who were escorting a small, lame man. He had his back to us, but when he turned, I saw it was Father Muhando. He was barefoot and stripped to the waist. He resembled a black Christ, carrying an invisible cross. I pushed my way through the crowd, and as I got nearer, called:

—*Father Muhando!*

—*They say it was I who set off the explosions.*

—*What nonsense! And didn't you explain?*

—*Yes, I explained. I confessed to everything.*

—*You confessed?*

—*Yes. It was I who blew up all these foreigners.*

I was overcome with shock. I looked at the Italian, who was taking his camera out of a plastic bag. By the time he managed to focus it, the prisoner was being taken into the administration building. A policeman warned the foreigner: no photographs. It wasn't the right time for them.

The Italian requested access to the room where the priest was being held. But Chupanga was firm. This was a matter of internal security. Affairs of state must have priority. Estêvão Jonas only allowed us to visit the prisoner the following morning.

Seated on a diviner's stool, Father Muhando was having his breakfast. As we approached him, I was surprised at his meal: the man was dipping his fried fish in his tea. He smiled:

—*Like this, the fish tastes sweet.*

He asked me to translate what he was saying to me. I explained it wasn't necessary, but he was adamant:

—*Translate!*

I found this strange: the man who was always indisposed now seemed to be in his seventh heaven. But when it came to it, he allowed me no time. He picked off his words as if on a string, like someone whose time was running out.

—*You look at me and think I'm crazy, a lunatickle. But it's all the same to me.*

—*For God's sake, I don't think anything*— retorted Massimo.

—*There's just one thing: you must never, but never, take a photo of me! And don't record me. Who are you to go around taking photos and recording without permission?*

The Italian hung his head and apologised. He seemed sincere. And so, with a look of concentration, he listened to the rest of the priest's talk. To begin with, Muhando listed his complaints: supposing, he suggested to the Italian, the opposite were the case. That is, a group of black Africans turned up in the middle of Italy, conducting inquiries, scouring through private matters. How would the Italians react?

Then, the priest appeared willing to provide information. But he was only pretending. For he explained: the soldier who exploded was an ugly man. His balls were bigger than a stallion's. You could even hear them clanging as he walked along. He was saying this, although he had never set eyes on them when they were alive. They had flown over the marula tree posthumously. And landed on the highway for all to see.

And he now recalled going to the *nyanga*, whom he referred to as a colleague, in order to lay the Zambian's private parts in their final resting place. For by this time, there were vultures circling over the huge canopy of the tree. It would be to invite disaster if those things were to be left like that, exposed to the creatures of the wild. Never again would there be any peace and quiet if the birds swallowed the foreigner's balls. Animals don't visit human flesh. At least, not without prior permission. And the priest:

—*Like you, sir, who visits us without asking*— he said, pointing to the Italian.

What had he and the witchdoctor done, then? They had picked the poor man's organs off the branches and laid them to rest far away in the depths of the bush, where only untamed creatures dwell.

—*We should leave you there too, sir.*

The Italian no longer found the story funny. The priest was a creature unworthy of credit. It confirmed what he had already heard about him: the priest had gone mad, and neglected his holy duties. On more than one occasion, he had been heard insulting God in public places. A child died, defenceless against suffering, and Muhando would march out of the church and challenge his Creator, insulting him in front of all and sundry. He would call him the worst names, pull him down a peg or two in no uncertain fashion.

—*Is it true that you insult God?*

—*Which God?*

—*Well … God.*

—*Ah! That one. Yes, it's true. I insult him when he misbehaves.*

He had his reasons for such intimacy – he and God were

colleagues, with knowledge of mutual secrets. When he drank, He drank too. That's why he didn't pray to God. Rather, he prayed with God.

—*Do you know where my real church is? Do you know? It's next to the river, down there among the reeds.*

He climbed on a box and peered out of the window. He called us over to look.

—*See. It's there that I talk with God.*

—*Why there?*

—*That's where God's footprints are.*

As far as Father Muhando was concerned, the reason why the place was holy was simple: in olden times, the Devil was dying. God got worried: without the Demon, he would only be a half. So that was when God hastened to cure his eternal foe. The first thing God did was to drink water. At that time, there was only the sea. He drank some of the salty water, full of algae and organisms. God began to have hallucinations and vomited all over the universe. His vomit was acid and living things wasted away, contaminated by the nauseating smell. The water grew stale, the plants turned yellow. Cows began to produce blood instead of milk. God was growing weaker and painful to see. That was when, already exhausted, he invented rivers. He created rivers with water brought from his most distant strengths, the veins of his soul. But he was weakened, incapable of vastness. That's why rivers are not as infinite as the sea. It was enough to set eyes on that fresh water for God's soul to be reinvigorated. However, the rivers were not enough in themselves. They needed the sea, the place of infinity. And so water returned to water.

—*God knelt down there, in that declivity*— said Muhando, pointing to the river. —*One knee on this side and the other on the far shore over there. And he bent over to quench his thirst.*

They say he drank and drank until the thirst of all the springs had been quenched. He looked at the firmament and closed the sun in his eyes. There was too much light: everything became a mirage. From his face, which had been momentarily blinded, emerged Man. This was to be the first man. From the eyes of God, injured by such brightness, a tear was shed. From the water of this tear, a woman was born. This was the first woman. And both Man and Woman wandered among the reeds on the banks of the rivers.

—*There, among the reeds: that's my church. That's where I bend over to look into the eyes of God. I speak to him through the water.*

The priest warned: everything they had heard about him was true. Yes indeed, it was all true. It was true that he paid visits to Hell. Although, strictly speaking, it was Hell that came to visit him. And those who controlled our fate were demons.

—*You need to consult one demon before you can find out where another demon lives.*

He gave, by way of example, the administrator. His stepson had killed people and sold drugs. That young fellow was the man who sucked blood from a vampire. Everyone knew. The boy was taking after his mother. The First Lady had got herself powers that no power could agree to. She had expelled the peasant farmers from the valley. The land belonging to the poorest had been turned over to her. It was common knowledge. But no one could do anything about what they knew.

—*They've already threatened me. Even God intimidated me. They go together like body and soul, those folk.*

Then, the priest asked us to gather round him. He wanted to share a secret. It was really very simple: he knew they were going to transfer him. All they needed was an excuse. They would send him to the city, where there are so many priests that they no longer have any importance at all.

—*I'm past caring anyway. I'm tired of this life. And like this, I get out of here with my fare paid.*

And turning to Massimo Risi, he gave him his blessing. It was his blessing and not the divine one. For he knew that Tizangara was beyond heavenly protection.

—*Take care, my son. Round here, losses are always greater than damages.*

We returned to the guesthouse. The priest's madness seemed to have left the foreigner crestfallen. He had a tendency to be melancholic at the best of times. The priest had talked a lot and said little. Massimo sat down in front of his report, chewing his pen. The page fell asleep without being written on.

I withdrew to the solitude of my room. I stayed awake for some time, thinking about the presence here of this Italian. Why did our country need inspectors from outside? What was it that had left us so discredited in the eyes of the world? One could hear Temporina's muffled song echoing down the corridor. The poor girl was keeping her ghosts at bay. Then, suddenly, I heard the Italian tapping on my door. He came in all agitated:

—*I can't sleep. I've had a terrible dream.*

He dreamed that he was returning to Europe and the same plane was carrying the coffins of the blue helmets who had died. When they landed, they were met by a full guard of honour. But when they were unloaded, the coffins were no more than tiny boxes, not much bigger than matchboxes. Nor did they need to be any bigger to hold what they were holding. Some minute flags had been draped over these little boxes. The sky blue of the United Nations. The widows passed by the stand where the caskets had been laid and each of them took the package that belonged to her and put it in her handbag. And finally, when they paid him their respects, Massimo noticed that they bent right over until they were next to the ground. They were huge, and it was only then that he realised he had turned into a midget. He had returned alive from Africa. But he had no size left.

As I looked at Massimo, it suddenly occurred to me that he really had shrunk abnormally. I signalled to him to keep quiet, and to listen to Temporina singing. The foreigner curled up tight, half asleep.

Until the young-old woman's voice fell silent. There, surrounded by darkness, I thought: there are creatures who live in their burrows and only leave the earth to die. I wished I was one of them. Without light and free of the sun's calendar. In shadow the whole time, mouth and eyes closed to the dust. When it was time to cross over beyond life, I would know how to dwell on the other side.

12   *Father dreaming before the unflowing river*

> *Do you want to know where the cat is?*
> *Well, look in the warmest corner.*
> (Proverb)

> *If you want to see in the night*
> *rinse your eyes with the water*
> *where the cat washed its eyes.*
> (A saying from Tizangara)

—*I'm going outside to hang up my bones.*

My father always announced what he had decided to do as he walked out of the door. He spoke as if he were alone. He'd been like that for many years. As his bones hurt him and he suffered from extreme tiredness, before he went to bed he would shed his skeleton so as to sleep better.

He'd been like that for nearly a lifetime. On the few nights we had spent together, it was always the same: we would eat in silence, according to his instruction. It was unlucky to talk during a meal. All that could be heard was the sound of fingers pinching up the flour, dipping it once, and then again, in the dry fish curry. And one could hear the sound of chewing, the loud chomping of jaws. After dinner, he would get up and declare his intention of unboning himself. He would step out into the darkness and only return when it was light, as fresh as the dew on an early morning leaf. I never followed him for fear that he might notice my suspicions. So I just assumed that it was another of his many lies. He had already left us puzzled with his wanderings. He lived on borrowed oaths.

He wasn't put out when we held him to account. He would answer by returning the question:

—*What is our body made of? Of flesh, blood, confined waters?*

No, according to him, one's body was made of time. When our allotted time was up, our body was finished too. And at the end of it all, what's left? Bones. The non-time, our mineral essence. If there's something we've got to look after, it's our skeleton, our timid, hidden eternity.

All this I remembered as we walked towards my old house. I was going to visit my old man, who had just taken possession of his old home again. Massimo insisted on going with me. I would rather he had left me alone, me and my private intentions. But the man confessed that he was scared of being left by himself in the guesthouse.

When we arrived, there was no immediate sign of old Sulpício. I called but there was no answer. I had almost made up my mind to leave when I decided to take a look in the back yard. In an African house, that's where everything happens. And indeed, that was the case. There he was, sitting back in his old chair. We announced ourselves. He sat there, silent, impassive, contemplating the river. When at last he spoke, I got a fright:

—*Can you hear the birds?*

There were no birds at all. Complete and utter silence reigned. But only my father could hear the raucous screech of the flamingos. It was his debt to those long-legged fowl. Fishermen call them 'life belts'. At dead of night during the height of a storm, when they have no idea how far they are from land, it is the presence and voice of the flamingos that guide lost fishermen.

My old man was also saved by those great birds. Washed overboard on some fishing trip, he was already drinking the ocean, swallowed up by the waves and spewed up by the night, when he caught sight of ghosts grazing the floor of the darkness. They were elusive white shapes along the line of surf. His heart's first feeling was:

—*God has sent me angels already!*

They weren't angels. They were in fact rose-coloured flamingos pecking at the carpet of seaweed. The incident confirmed the vocation of these birds as saviours. Ever since then, my old man had retained the cry of these creatures, and would return to the memory every time he felt lost. At that moment, for example, there in the yard of our home, there was little likelihood of flamingos. But there he was contemplating them, flying in the direction of our house. That was the direction of good omens.

Our arrival had merely interrupted his visions. In his annoyance, my old man growled the moment he saw us:

—*Get out of here.*

—*Give us your welcome, father.*

Pressing his hands down on his knees, the old man got up from his chair. He confronted me angrily:

—*Where is it you're sleeping?*

He didn't give me time to answer. His questions came at me in cascades: why had I abandoned our home? Why had I agreed to work for that evil bastard Estêvão Jonas? Why was I sticking my nose in where it wasn't wanted?

—*Father, calm down. We live in peaceful times now.*

—*When the water's calm, that's when a man drowns.*

He passed his hand over his head, smoothing his hair from the back to the front. He had to make an effort not to shout.

—*And now, you bring me this white man.*

He said he knew what they were like, whites. When they arrived, they were full of sweet talk. But it didn't work with him. He would keep quiet. That European wasn't going to enter his soul through any words he uttered. Massimo Risi, full of velvety manners, implored him:

—*But Senhor Sulplício ...*

—*Don't say my name! Never do that again!*

I knew the basis of this principle: a person's name is intimate, like a being within a being. Authorisation had to be given for someone to utter another person's name. As far as he was concerned, the Italian was guilty of nothing less than an invasion. Old Sulplício used me to deliver a message to the European:

—*Tell him I won't have it.*

Massimo stood there, impotent, unable to move, rooted to the ground, without anywhere to go. Meanwhile, it had begun to rain. As always, my father didn't shelter from the rain. Drops ran down the lines in his face. He tasted some of them, and concluded:

—*This rain's too old.*

It's always raining the same rain, he was wont to say. Except that it only does it now and then. But it's always the same rain. Old Sulplício's stories. He was waiting for a fresh new rain, one that had just made its appearance. When that happened, this world would turn a few somersaults, and prospects would be better.

He looked at the sky scornfully. He glanced at us with a similar look of superiority. Then he sat down again and sank back into his previous indifference. Stock still, under the rain. We stood there silently, waiting for a change in his mood. I watched my father in his obstinacy and thought I distinguished in him an entire race establishing its time against the time of the others. For the first time, I felt proud of him. I even hoped he wouldn't talk. There he was before the river, in a chair that was as ancient as the ground itself. He barely moved, his eyes as absent as those of a crocodile. For him, the river was the only confirmation that he was alive. After a while, when he seemed to be asleep, he asked:

—*Has the river stopped?*

The Italian looked at me, flabbergasted. I knew it wasn't a question that required an answer. After all, he wasn't speaking what he was saying. He was referring to something else. Every object has the right to be a word. It is the duty of each word not to be nothing at all. The matter he was referring to was time. Like the river: when it's unflowing, that's when time grows.

—*Has the river stopped? Has it?*

—*No, father.*

—*Not yet? Well, when it does stop, then I'll talk to this foreigner.*

We gave up. We went inside the house. My father joined us and settled down in a corner, his mat covering some large sheets of paper. He stretched painfully. That night, he wouldn't hang his bones out. He didn't trust the darkness round there. We fell asleep in the living room. We woke up with a start. My father was shouting into our ears. He was upbraiding me for serving the very people who had destroyed him. The Italian for having insinuated himself into someone else's soul.

—*That man there, whose white is he?*

Whose? I explained who Massimo was, sure that he was hardly listening. I urged him to calm down. But he kept on shouting.

He was talking to me as if the Italian weren't there. But it was Massimo Risi he was addressing. He talked hurriedly and all in a muddle: for centuries, they'd wanted us to be European, to accept their way of life. There were even some who imitated whites, faded blacks. But he, if he was to be one of them, would have done the job properly from head to toe. He would have gone to Europe and asked for a position right there in the middle of Portugal. They wouldn't let him? How come? You're either Portuguese or you aren't, isn't that so? So do you invite someone into your house and park the fellow in the back, somewhere fit for domestic animals? Same family, same house. Isn't that true?

—*Or isn't it a fact that this white man is sleeping on the best mattress in the house?*

—*Father: please don't get angry. This man has nothing to do with it.*

—*Your problem is that what you know has little age.*

—*I know what went on in the old days. I remember things ...*

—*You remember, but you don't know anything.*

Did I know, for instance, how hard he'd toiled? Did I know what he did for a living before I was even born? Well, during those years, he worked as a game warden. It was in colonial times and you didn't muck around. He was practically the only black man to hold such a position. It hadn't been easy.

—*I suffered racism of one type or another. I swallowed a toad's saliva.*

He had learned, in military service, that you only fired on the enemy when he was near. But in his case, he was so near that he ran the risk of shooting himself. Or he might have to admit: the enemy was inside him. The target he was firing at was not a foreign country, but a province of himself. The Portuguese flag wasn't his. That much he knew.

—*But consider this: what other flag did I have?*

And if there were, if there were another flag, there wasn't another flagpole except for the one where the Portuguese flag was hoisted. Was he making himself clear? It was that my mother would never have accepted that he had fought for the colonials. She, for her part, heaped praise on the guerrillas who fought for independence. As if no one from that group was impure.

But hardly had he opened his mouth than I guessed the rest. For he said things crossways, looking at me but addressing the other. Only after some time did he turn to Massimo and address him directly:

—*I'll only say one thing to you.*

He stopped, as if he had suddenly forgotten what it was. Then he gained a new decisiveness, and issued a command:

—*Come with me.*

We got up and followed in silence. My old man led the way, walking resolutely through the early morning mist and the half-light. His firm step gave him a military bearing. Nothing less than more, nothing more than less. He entered the shade of the tamarind tree and showed us something in his hands.

—*Look!*

We peered in vain. His hands were empty. But he coolly rolled up his sleeves to reveal two parallel scars running up from his wrists. His fingers had paid for it dearly – for years they had moved slowly in a tortoise-like arc.

—*They tied me to that tree. They bound me with rope, and poured salt on my wounds.*

—*Who?*

—*Those same people you are trying to help now.*

By now, I was familiar with Sulplício's arguments. When the people from the Revolution got here, they said we would become the owners and the bosses. Everyone was happy. My mother, she was very happy. But Sulplício was full of fear. Kill the boss? It's more difficult to kill the slave that dwells within us. Now, there was neither boss nor slave.

—*We've just changed boss.*

—*But what happened?*

What happened? He was a guard way back in colonial times. Couldn't we understand? A black like him serving the white forces? Did we know what he had gone through? And yet he had no complaints, he had suffered, and then suffered again. But a person isn't like corn that dies and stays upright. At least he still had some power to refuse: not to speak when others asked him to. The Italian pressed him:

—*So what happened then? With your hands ...*

I was well acquainted with the episode and thought it best to shorten the story. I remembered the incident only too well. It happened after Jonas took power as administrator. On one occasion, my old man caught Jonas's stepson red-handed hunting elephant. It wasn't the season and he had no licence. So he arrested him. That was his mistake. Dona Ermelinda, the chief's wife, turned up at the prison complaining that it was a question of political persecution.

—*Let my son go*— the First Lady ordered.

Sulplício didn't obey the order. Ermelinda pressed on obstinately:

—*You're persecuting our family!*

Not long afterwards, the administrator arrived. The tables were turned. In an instant, the boy was free, and he, the warden, was under arrest, his hands bound. His other colleagues tied him up, quick to obey orders. The knot was far too tight. Sulplício protested that the rope was stopping the blood from circulating to his hands. To no avail. None of his colleagues made a move to defend him. It was Dona Ermelinda who added insult to injury by pouring salt on the rope. And she ordered them to leave him tied up until the following day.

—*And you, my son, still frequent such people.*

Sulpício went back to the veranda that looked over the river. He now no longer wanted any visitors at all. At least unless they were the angels that flew across the sky at sunset. But for the rest, he just wanted to be left alone. He leaned against a trunk and spoke to me:

—*I can look after myself, boy. I can look after myself!*

—*Don't worry, father. We'll leave you alone soon.*

—*Yes, and take that foreigner with you. Before you go, I want to tell you something: it's a very good thing.*

—*What's a very good thing, father?*

—*That you're a translator.*

And he gave me an explanation I had never heard before. I was a special son: ever since I was very young, my father had noticed that the gods spoke through my mouth. This, because as a young child, I suffered from grave illnesses. At such times, death occupied my body, but never got as far as carrying me off. According to local wisdom, such resistance was a sign: I had the gift of translating words from the dead. This was the translation I had been doing ever since I was born. It was my vocation therefore to be a translator.

—*That's why you must take care, Senhor Massimo—* the old man said. —*Do you hear me?*

—*Say that again, Senhor Sulpício.*

—*Be careful: your words may burn my son's mouth. Do you understand?*

—*Yes, I understand.*

—*Now go, for I've already spent a lot of time with you.*

He waved us away. He wanted to be alone again. Just as we were leaving, we heard another explosion in the distance. We rushed back to where old Sulplício was. Impassive, his attention was still immersed in the eternity of the river.

—*Didn't you hear it, father?*

He gestured me to come nearer. With another gesture, he told the Italian to keep his distance. I put my ear up against his face. At that point, he said:

—*That was one of the other explosions.*

—*The other? What other?*

And then, laconically, he explained: it was a lie that only foreign soldiers were exploding. According to him, there were other explosions that killed our people. True explosions, with evidence of blood and tears. Such as the one that had just occurred.

—*Father, tell me what you know …*

He waved his arm in a gesture of refusal: nothing, he had already said too much.

—*You know something, son? A mouth never talks alone. Maybe in that white fellow's homeland. But here, no.*

—*I beg you to tell me. Just me.*

—*Learn one thing, my son. In our country, one man is all the others.*

He wasn't going to talk, I could tell. All the more so given the company I was keeping. It wasn't that he disliked the visitor. But it would be better if they remained divorced, out of common dissent. He had sworn to himself first and foremost never even to say half of what he knew. But it wouldn't always be like that. I knew him. His heart had weak hands: everything he loved ended up flowing into nothingness. It was worse now because of his cut wrists. He had lost his energy, and lost his belief. My father would indeed talk. But through the voice of others.

13   *The dimwit's demise*

Life is a sweet kiss in a bitter mouth.
(The witchdoctor's statement)

That morning, when we arrived at the guesthouse, we were surprised by the sound of weeping. It was coming from Temporina's room. We found her bowed over a wash-basin. She looked as if she had been sick. But no: she was merely taking care that her tears should not fall on the floor. It's said that a bewitched woman's tears cause the strangest things to spring from the soil. We stood there respectfully, waiting for her tears to flow from her face into the white basin. Then she wiped her face with her hands and spoke:

—*They've killed my brother.*

Her only brother, the simpleton who had inherited Hortensia's assets. It was a sad piece of news and added a new element to that whole story. The lad had been blown up. This time, however, it was a real explosion, the type we'd got used to during the war. As straightforward as it was cruel: the boy had stepped on a mine and his legs had become separated from his body as if he were a rag doll in shreds. Before any help could reach him, he had bled to death. The Italian shook me nervously.

—*That was the explosion we heard yesterday at your father's house.*

In an act of sudden decisiveness, Temporina wrapped a *capulana* over her skirt and declared:

—*I'm going out!*

—*You can't, Temporina.*

I got as far as grabbing her arm. But I couldn't hold her. She disappeared down the corridor. I tried to follow on her heels. In vain: she had already vanished among the streets. I returned to Massimo Risi's room and once again had that feeling of foreboding that had afflicted me on the occasion of the first explosion. On the Italian's bed, there was a jumble of papers. In his despair, Massimo was rummaging through the pile.

—*Look!*

He pointed to the scattered papers and photos. —*Look, look,* he repeated. I picked up one or two loose sheets. They were blank.

—*There's nothing written here.*

—*Exactly. And look at the photos!*

They were sheets of photographic paper, but they were blank. That was the mystery – those papers and those images were not virgin. Up until then, they had been defiled by letters, by graven images. All this was the proof, the evidence that the Italian had accumulated to show to his superiors.

—*Has it all been erased?*

—Are you sure that these aren't different sheets?

Massimo held his head in his hands:

—I'm going mad, I can't stand this anymore.

He complained of a splitting headache. I suggested we went outside to get some fresh air. But the Italian didn't have time for strolls. We'd go out, yes, but in the direction of the administration building to see if there was any news.

On the way, we had an extraordinary encounter: Father Muhando, now free, wandering along the streets shouting. We tried to stop him, but he shook us off. He was berating God, like one possessed. It was unforgivable that He should have taken the nameless dimwit child. He would get His comeuppance down here on Earth, for it would be too late if it was left until he got to Heaven. The Italian was astonished: so the priest had abandoned his imprisonment, forsaken the dream of escape?

—There's no real prison here— I explained to the Italian.

At the entrance to the building, we met Zeca Andorinho, the most powerful witchdoctor in the area. The man was furtively leaving the administrator's office to fulfil the orders he had been given. Every time the world shook, he was to pass by the chief's house to cleanse the place, exorcising evil spirits.

Zeca Andorinho signalled to us to follow him and walked on, his face hidden. We followed at some distance until he paused in the safety of a shadow. When he saw us, he stared at the foreigner as if he recognised him. At first, he spoke in his own language. He did this deliberately, for he knew how to speak Portuguese. Only after he'd spoken a few sentences did he address the Italian in Portuguese.

—*I've seen you before.*

—*It must have been around here—* answered Massimo Risi.

—*No, I've seen you in my house.*

—*That's impossible. I've never been there—* and looking at me for confirmation: —*have we ever been there?*

—*Come in, for this light will make your headache even worse.*

Massimo was disturbed. How did this man know about his migraine?

—*Come into the darkness here and you'll feel a bit better.*

We were at the entrance to one of Andorinho's two houses. Massimo went in, and stood waiting for the other to tell him what to do. The witchdoctor told him to stretch out his legs and take his shoes off. This time, I really had to translate. The witchdoctor had stopped talking in Portuguese. He went over to speaking the local tongue, expressing himself with his eyes closed.

—*There's a woman who came to see me.*

—*What woman?*

—*She asked me to do a job for her.*

I made a sign to the Italian not to say anything. The witchdoctor was past paying him any attention. The old man, with his eyes half-closed, seemed to change the subject on a whim. He said there were spells called *likaho*. A whole variety of such spells, each one made from a different animal. There was a lizard *likaho*: it made a man's belly swell. The same thing happened to those who were ambitious – such folk were devoured by their stomach. There was an ant *likaho*, and the victims grew thinner and thinner until they were the size of the insect. The Italian glanced at me out of the corner of his eye and I guessed his fear. Could that be the spell that had visited him during his nightmare? Zeca Andorinho paused, as if he were pondering a confession. Then he spoke:

—*Now, this* likaho *that's afflicting the soldiers is that of a toad.*

—*A toad?*

—*They grow fatter and fatter until they're the size of a baobab. And when they can no longer contain themselves, they burst.*

He did this spell to order for the men of Tizangara. The locals were jealous of the visitors. They envied their wealth, which was paraded in order to make their wives go dizzy. They had no way of punishing the foreign males for their lingering looks. Especially if they wore the uniform of the soldiers from the United Nations.

—*That was the spell I used against these locusts.*

Massimo already knew: these locusts were the blue helmets. So this spell began where all men begin – in courtship. As the victim of the spell continued, he got hotter and his body lost control. He swelled up without being aware of it. He grew like a toad in the face of its own fear. Until at the precise moment of orgasm, he exploded.

The witchdoctor opened his eyes at last, and returned to the room as if he had just arrived. He stared at the foreigner and smiled at him:

—*Now, let me ask you an awkward question.*

—*By all means do.*

—*Did you make love to that old-young girl at the hotel ...*

—*No, I only dreamed it.*

—*Tell me man to man, did you really only dream it? Didn't anything happen to your clothes?*

The Italian remained silent. There was a question clearly etched on his face: why, then, hadn't he exploded? But he was so frightened that he couldn't say a word. The witch-doctor answered his unasked question.

—*You received some treatment.*

—*Treatment?*

—*You've been immunised. I cast a tortoise* likaho *on you. To protect you.*

—*You cast a spell on me? And why did you do that?*

—*It was a woman who asked me to vaccinate you.*

Massimo mixed fear with apprehension, terror with alarm. Fear of the unknown, apprehension about believing, terror of illness, alarm at spells. All he could do was to repeat:

—*A woman?*

—*Don't insist, brother.*

—*But which woman?*

—*Forget it: you'll never know.*

—*I'm going to ask one more time: which woman?*

—*Don't you want to find out about those fellows who exploded? Well, switch on your machine because I'm going to tell you about the case of the Zambian. And the others as well. Turn your recorder on, then. But while we're on the subject, haven't you brought me a little bottle to help loosen my tongue?*

14 The witchdoctor Andorinho's talk

It's the stray dog that finds the bone.
(Proverb)

*What do I know about the unmasted Zambian? And the
Pakistani? And all the others who exploded? Do you want to
know how they were put out of service? Well, Your Excellency:
every man drops what he can't hold. I, Zeca Andorinho, make
sure I hold on to my dependencies. You won't find me blowing
my own trumpet. You know something, sir: everything falls,
even the clouds drop from the sky. Who's to blame for this?
No one. I'm serious, sir. I don't know what happened with all
due respect for my ignorance. When we are born, we know
everything, but don't remember anything. Then we grow up,
and we start gaining memory, while our knowledge shrinks.
But even as a witchdoctor, in this particular matter, I have
neither memory nor knowledge. It's the angels who are all-
seeing witnesses. You'd do better to interview them. Interview
the angels, my dear sir. They won't refuse to talk to someone
like you.*

I'll confess one thing, though, so help me God: I don't like the ways of these foreigners nowadays. In olden times, these distant visitors would pass through and rub themselves against our girls. But they didn't carry off anyone they took a fancy to. We chose among ourselves the most takeable lasses. Not anymore. Nowadays a stranger becomes a husband in a trice, with no father-in-law or brother-in-law, illegal in their respect for the old way of life. I can see you, sir, don't think I can't see you. Your eyes are fishing for beautiful girls. Your net has got caught under a deep rock. That woman used a fish to catch your bait, I'll tell you that much, brother.

A secret: it was all a lie about Temporina. She wasn't a virgin. I only found out later — she'd had an affair with the priest. Yes, it had all happened in the dark, behind the curtains. Muhando had always managed to find some use for the church. To hide his love affairs from the envious looks of those whom love had ignored. So you can relax, my dear Massimo. That scaly skin won't last for ever. It's a fleeting thing. One day, without anyone noticing it, something akin to what happens to snakes will occur — she will become descaled, ready for some new summer.

Listen to me, sir: I'm living the rough draft of a life, getting a few morsels of future for myself. It's because here in the town, no one will guarantee us anything. Not even the land, which is the exclusive property of the gods, not even the land is spared the effects of greed. Nothing is ours nowadays. One of those foreigners turns up, either a local one or one from outside, and snatches everything away from us all in one go. Even the ground on which we stand is snatched away. I say this because I've seen it with my own eyes: I don't trust anybody, we're being pushed to where there's no true place nor time.

For example: some days ago, Jonas, the administrator, gave me the order to put an end to the explosions. I refused. Politely, but I refused. Well, why should I obey the order of someone like Jonas? Here in Tizangara? He's a foreigner, just like you, sir. I only obey other powers. Like you, sir, who doesn't answer to us. Your bosses are outside, aren't they? Well, mine are even further outside. Do you get me?

Living is easy: even the dead manage it. But life is a burden that has to be borne by all living creatures. Life, dear sir, is a sweet kiss on a bitter mouth. Be careful of them, my friend. Some don't live for fear of dying, I don't die for fear of living. Do you understand, sir? Time here is all about survival. It's not like there, where you're from. Here, the only people who get to the future are those who live life at a slow pace. The only thing that tires us is chasing away evil spirits. I'm not trying to be clever. Wait, and I'll explain myself.

I talk such things about our present leaders. I shouldn't talk, much less with you, an outsider from foreign parts. But I talk even so. For such leaders should be like a great tree that provides shade. But they've got more roots than leaves. They take a lot and give a little. Take that cursed stepson of the administrator. I've made sure he'll come to a sticky end: the boy's going to die of all that hurried wealth.

There are those who doubt my powers over such ways of life. And they ask — can it be that the hyena has turned into a goat? But I too can ask: is it the neck that carries the head or vice versa? Well, this lad is going to learn his lesson — the almond is going to crush the ant. I'm telling you, sir, and you'll see for yourself: the chief's stepson is going to have to gather wood if he wants to heat the saucepan. But that's a matter for us, let's leave it at that.

Now then, you ask me about these soldiers who've disappeared. You ask me if the Zambian soldier died. Did he die? Well, he died relatively. How come? Are you asking me how one dies relatively? I don't know, I can't explain it to you. I'd have to speak in my own language. And that's something not even this young lad can translate. For what has to be said has no words in any language. The only speech I've got is for what I invent. For I, my fine sir, am something like an alligator: I'm ugly and lumbering, but I lay an egg as if I were a little bird. On the other hand, I have my differences in relation to such creatures. My teeth are no good at scaring. On the contrary: my teeth are for others to bite me with. I offer facilities to my enemies. Can you see the type of education I had? There's a lot of talk about colonialism. But that's something I doubt ever existed. What those whites did was to occupy us. It wasn't just the land: they occupied our very selves, they set up camp right inside our heads. We're timber that's been left out in the rain. Now, we're no good for firewood or for providing shade. We've got to dry out in the light of a sun that doesn't yet exist. That sun can only be born within us. Are you following me?

Let's take things bit by bit. Who do you suspect? Me? Do you suspect the prostitute? It's clear you were never a whore. No offence meant. It's because this tale of the explosions can only undermine any advantages she may have. It's not good for her business.

Work it out for yourself: what's left of those who've been blown up? A leg? An eye? An ear? The only thing left is their dick. Yes, all the rest vanishes into thin air. Now, I've seen a man without a cock. But a cock without a man, I'm sorry. You're looking at me awkwardly. Let me ask you something else: can anyone drain the sea of all its water? It's the same thing, precisely the same thing. You can't drain all the blood from a body. So let me ask you yet another question: what happened to the blood of those who were blown to pieces? Where did it get to, for not a drop was left? You, sir, who are a whitish man, you don't know the answers.

And I'll tell you something else. That Anna Godwilling woman, she's the one who sees to the funerals of those cocks. Yes, she's the one who carries them off and gives them an honourable burial. The poor soul's sanity has been shattered. One less cock is one more reason for mourning, and every explosion makes her a widow. By now, the woman has planted a whole cemetery. The graves vary in size, and only she knows where each one is. I speak from experience, and with these eyes that will one day be eaten by the earth. The cocks were buried in accordance with the law here: pointing westwards, laid on their side. Balls all undamaged, each next to the other, its twin brother.

I've nearly finished. All I'm going to do is offer you a warning: as you walk along, watch where you tread. I made a tortoise likaho *to protect you. But never, never step any old how. The earth has its secret paths. Do you catch my drift? You, sir, read the book, while I read the ground.*

And finally, a word of advice. It's that there are questions which can't be directed to people, but to life. Ask life, sir. But not this side of life. For life doesn't end on the side of the living. It extends beyond, to the side of the dead. Seek out this other side of life, sir.

I've spoken. All that's left for me to do is to bring my speech to a close. And as no one wants to wish me well, I'll do it myself: may I live longer than the pangolin that falls from the sky whenever it rains.

15 The tamarind tree

What flies after it has died?
It's the leaf of a tree.
(A saying from Tizangara)

I couldn't resist it. I returned to my old house and there, under the shade of the tamarind, I submerged myself in memories. I looked at its huge canopy and thought to myself: we never owned the tamarind. It was the other way round, it was the tree that owned the house. It spread, unchecked, over the yard, raising the cement floor. I looked at the paving, wrinkled by roots, pushed up in thin slabs, and it seemed to me like a reptile changing its skin.

The tamarind together with its shadow: it was all designed to nurture longing. My childhood built its nest in that tree. On my child's afternoons, I would climb to the topmost branch as if on a giant's shoulder and oblivious to earthly concerns. I would gaze up at the sky's cultivations: plantations of clouds, a trace of a bird. And I would watch the flamingos streak across the sky like arrows. My father would sit down below, on the gnarled roots, and point up at the birds:

—*Look, there goes another!*

The flamingo seemed to linger in its passage overhead. Then my mother would call us, me to climb down and my father to go in.

—*What a man, what a man*— she would complain.

—*Leave father be, mother.*

—*It's just that I'm so alone in caring for our lives!*

My old man hadn't always been at such a loose end, lazing around to such an extent. There was a time when he toiled hard, working with animals out there in the furthest bush. But work hadn't been good to him. Before and after Independence, he had reaped a bitter harvest. Then he had sunk into that apathy, sitting there by the bend in the river. To my mother's sadness, for she would sigh:

—*Your father lacks behaviour.*

Old Sulplício would make little of this: your mother's like a cricket – she's allergic to silence. And she was wrong if she thought he wasn't doing anything. For according to him, he was run off his feet.

—*I'm busy learning bird language.*

What he liked was the ripeness of green mangoes. The sun, he said, ripens overnight. What could he do? Some things make a man, others a human being. And he sighed: time is the eternal builder of olden days. For example, he, Sulplício himself. It was an error of destiny – he had been a policeman in colonial times. When Independence came, he was put on the shelf, viewed as one who had betrayed his race.

That was when that Estêvão Jonas had arrived in Tizangara. He wore a guerrilla fighter's uniform and people looked at him as if he were a little god. He had left his homeland to take up arms and fight the colonists. My mother admired him greatly. At that time, so folks say, he wasn't like he is today. He was a man who devoted his time to others, he was capable of generosities. He had left for beyond the frontier knowing that he might never return. He had set off carrying his pain with him and returned bearing a dream. And he dreamed of embellishing futures, banishing poverty from the home.

—*This country will be great.*

My mother recalls him declaiming such hopes. When I was born, my father had already stopped being a game warden. And Estêvão Jonas had stopped dreaming of great futures. What was it that had died inside him? With Estêvão the following happened: his life forgot his promise. Today gobbled up yesterday. With my father, the opposite occurred – he wanted to live outside time. The rest I couldn't understand. My father left home when I was still less than a child. But he didn't leave town. He remained on the riverbank, next to the bend in the river. Among the same rushes where Father Muhando had discovered his holy place. Every time I ran into my old man, he seemed distant. He was no longer himself. He couldn't bear people asking him how he felt. Then he would bitterly blame the world.

—*And the land, our land, has anyone asked if it's feeling well?*

Sulplício loved Tizangara with filial devotion. As the war dragged on, many fled to the capital. Even the authorities fled to a secure place. Estêvão Jonas, for example, had hurriedly taken refuge in the big city. On the other hand, my father always declared: he would only leave his refuge after the bats had left his roof. He had become stuck to the walls like a piece of moss.

Now, sitting in the ample shade of the tamarind, I closed my eyes and summoned my yearnings. What did I see? A yard, but not that one. For in that patch of ground, there was a child. In that child's hands, my memory touched some items of sadness, insignificant little things encountered among the rubbish. With a child's skill, it was possible to make a toy out of such things. With a magician's gifts, he could turn the world into a game one could take to pieces again at the end. And what was this toy? That's what I couldn't make out in my dream. All that came to my hazy memory was the sight of a child hiding the toy among the roots of the tamarind.

I opened my eyes, startled by a noise. It was my father approaching.

—*What are you looking for?*

—*For nothing.*

He signalled to me to wait. He bent down among the branches and took something out.

—*Could it be this you're looking for?*

Yes, it was my old toy. I walked over slowly to disentangle the object. And finally, when I had it in my hands, I guessed its shape: it was a flamingo. Using wire and cloth, I had built the flying creature my mother had imagined in her story. The toy now seemed too much for my hands. I threw the doll upwards, the pink and white feathers scattered through the air, taking an eternity to fall to the ground. My old man picked one of them up and caressed it between his fingers.

That re-encounter with my childhood lent me unexpected courage, and without any prior thought I suddenly asked:

—*Am I really your son?*

—*Whose son are you then?*

—*I don't know, mother ...*

—*Mothers, mothers. What did she tell you?*

—*Nothing, father. She never told me anything.*

—*Well, I'm going to tell you something ...*

And he fell silent. He choked on his voice, as if it had given up halfway down his throat. He tried to start again, but gave up a second time. He passed his hands over his neck as if he were clearing his voice from the outside. After an infinity, he spoke once more:

—*You're my son. And never doubt it again.*

He tapped his lips with his fingers, as if to seal his words. He could even tell me how I'd been conceived. I hadn't been conceived immediately, at the outset of the marriage. Nor at one go. Whenever he and my mother made love, the sky unleashed heavy rain. The couple continued to make love under the deluge. As if there were no world and no rain. They had their reasons: for they had been making their one and only first child for years without end. They loved each other without pause. Every time their bodies crossed, they would say they were making another little piece of their coming child's body.

—*Tonight let's make his eyes.*

And as this was what they had decided to produce on that night, they chose somewhere in the full light of the moon to make love. They chose a piece of empty ground right under the moon. And so that's what they did, moonlit, continuing their task of making their child. How long did they take to do this? He shrugged his shoulders: a whole child can take longer than a life.

—*Do you understand me, son? You were conceived over my whole life.*

Doubt suddenly afflicted me: Sulplício was imagining that story at that precise moment. He was manufacturing a descendant out of me. He was eternalising himself, albeit as an illusion. But I accepted it. After all, everything is belief. Suddenly, he changed the subject completely:

—*And the foreigner?*

—*Massimo? He stayed at the guesthouse.*

—*Never let him tell you what to do.*

I could go around with him, for to go around with a white might bring me respect. But to be pushed around, never. Even the whites in the past never governed. In our weakness, we just gave them the illusion they were governing us.

—*Not even these ones now, these brothers of ours, colonists in spirit, govern as they think they do.*

Suddenly, he grew tired of spinning conversation and began to take his leave. But before doing so, he warned me:

—*They left some papers on the table for you.*

—*Who?*

—*That trickster Chupanga. He said he didn't want to leave them at the guesthouse because of that Italian.*

I opened the envelope. For the first time, I felt very afraid as I read the administrator's handwriting. As if his words were spying on me.

16   The return of the nation's heroes

A man's urine always falls near him.
(Proverb)

Comrade Excellency

The operative obligation of this report is the urgency of the situation in this locality, in the context of the explosive occurrences and occurrences of explosion. The situation in itself is of the most serious gravity, and outside the control of the political-administrative structures. We suspect enemy sabotage, designed to discredit us utmostly before the world community. I went so far as to suspect that priest, Father Muhando. He was even arrested under my orders. But he is incapable of anything. The one I do suspect is Anna Godwilling, whose existence has caused great expense in the heart of the popular masses. Indeed, this woman merits a paragraph.

She is a low-lifer, a woman bought off the peg, whose body has been patronised by most of the male public. This Anna has even sown confusion concerning my life, causing infelicitous gossip about my worthy behaviour. These rumours have spread across the town and the grass hut areas. It is true, even the hut dwellers talk about me. It is just as you put it, Comrade Excellency: the masses bear wounds on their back, the chiefs bear them on their brow. What is the purpose and objective of this Anna woman? For me, it is vengeance. Do not forget that she was arrested and transferred to a re-education camp on the occasion of Operation Production. Or it may be because of an affair with me, an involvement that was unsatisfactorily resolved. One of those neverlasting loves.

My esteemed Ermelinda never ceases to insist that I should arrest Anna Godwilling. My lady wife holds the woman in the greatest hatred. To her, it is all crystal clear: it is the prostitute who is the cause of the explosions. That I know everything but pretend there is no proof. And yet, let me ask: how can I put her in gaol, as if our country were a land of inhuman rights? And what is worse, with these foreign folk sniffing at us?

I am exceedingly concerned, to the point of panic. That Italian, the priest, the witchdoctor and all the rest. What do they want? Where will they stop? The other day, I even had a dream. We were carrying out the ceremonies to summon our heroes from the past. Tzunguine came, Madiduane and the others who fought the colonists. We sat down with them and asked them to place some order in our world today, to expel the new colonists who have caused such suffering among our people. That same night, I woke with Tzunguine and Madiduane shaking me and ordering me to get up.

—What are you doing, my heroes?

—Didn't you ask us to expel the oppressors?

—Yes, I did.

—Well, we're expelling you.

—Me?

—You and the other abusers of power.

You see? That was my dream, my disgrace. For Your Comrade Excellency was also there. Booted out like me. The rebels of our glorious History kicking us out of History? But the worst thing about this nightmare was the following: the heroes threatened my stepson Jonassane that if he did not return the lands he was occupying, they would cause him to disappear. And isn't that just what happened? The following day, by this time outside the dream and in the midst of real life, there was no sign of my stepson. It would seem that the lad had fled to the neighbouring country. And what was more, he had taken some of my savings with him. Is that the work of explicable forces?

And now, Excellency, begging your pardon, I am going to self-criticise you. For we, after all, have been hurling blasphemies against our ancestors. That is what I say: otherwise how can we explain the unbelievable things that have happened? For example, last week a male donkey gave birth to a child. A person with skin and hair like mine and Your Excellency's was born. I beg your pardon, I should not have mingled the dignity of your name with matters relating to donkeys or non-donkeys. But that is exactly what happened, a baby born from an animal. And what was even more uncanny: the child was born wearing military boots. It was a shock of the highest order. The reporter from the local radio even wanted to do a news item on it, but I refused to allow it.

Such things shame us in terms of civilisation and democracy. Not to mention the prestige of our glorious armed forces, represented there by a pair of boots and laces. We have enough tittle-tattle to contend with because of these wretched explosions.

I was called upon to confirm the truth of the incident with the donkey. But I refused. I confess, Excellency: I was frightened. For what if it was a factually authenticated truth? How could one reconcile the explanation for such a thing in the context of current ideas? Or even according to the old Marxist–Leninist conjuncture? Do you know what I say? Repairs have been carried out in the sky, and only rust has been falling from the clouds. God forgive you, most excellent sir. Let me ask one thing, Excellency: are you dreaming legally? Yes, do your dreams match your head? The problem is that with me, it doesn't happen. I wake up full of twitches, and pulling wry faces. I'll tell you this to release the weight from my sub-conscience: I've turned into a face-puller, I'm like one of those drunkards who wander along with no place to go.

I have analysed your last letter and agree fully with your most enlightened opinion: it is indeed a problem that I am from the South, and do not speak the language here. But the fact that my wife is a legitimate local can help. Given the length of these lines, I shall proceed no further, but salute your firm leadership in the affairs of state and the capitalist transformations currently being implemented in favour of the popular masses.

P.S. – As an addendum, I have a confession to make: my wife, yes even she has been behaving a little strangely. For one afternoon, she went to attend one of those ceremonies the local people have. She went. My word of honour, Excellency. The fact that she went is serious in itself. But she didn't just attend. She danced, sang and prayed. True, Excellency, and it wasn't she who told me, but it was reported by the security guards. She arrived home late at night, and displaying a shameful fatigue. She said nothing, ate nothing, nothing at all. All of a sudden, she let out a sigh, and in a voice I'd never heard before, said:

—Husband, tonight yet another soldier is going to explode.

And do you want to know the worst? It was no sooner said than undone. For on that very night, another accident occurred involving one of those United Nationalists. The fellow dissolved completely, he didn't even leave any dust, as God is my witness. How do I interpret such attitudes? It occurred to me that Ermelinda might have some involvement in the matter. But my suspicion came and went. I can't imagine putting the mother of the son of her former husband in prison.

What can I do? Transfer my own spouse to the capital? Have her committed and put out of harm's way until she's passed fifty? I am writing crookedly in straight lines, and beg your forgiveness for my openness. Together with the bearer of this letter, I am sending you the goat meat you asked for and one or two jars of palm liquor. There are seven animals and twenty-five units of drink. Please check this so as not to tempt any middle-ranking cadre to indulge in diversions.

17 *The bird in the crocodile's mouth*

It's not enough to have a dream.
I want to be a dream.
(Anna Godwilling's words)

I went into Massimo's room and a mass of papers was spread across every item of furniture.

—*Don't tell me the letters have faded again?!*

—*No.*

Then, I felt a chill. The Italian was packing up his things. He was going. An unexpected sadness darkened my world. Was I beginning to like the foreigner?

—*Are you leaving?*

The man confirmed this with no more than a slight nod. I taunted him: was he going to give up, throw it all in? Was he going to abandon his ambition for promotion just like that, when he was only halfway?

—*What way?*

I didn't know how to answer. He was right. At the very least, it was a labyrinth. The longer he stayed there, the more lost he would become. And so, as he packed his clothes tidily in his case, the foreigner seemed to be folding his own soul. At a certain point, he stopped, with a strange smile. Why was he laughing?

—*Didn't you tell me I should tell stories? Well, I've just remembered one.*

—*A story at last! Let's hear it, Massimo.*

—*It's not a story, it's a recollection. I remember what they used to do with my grandfather, when he grew old in Italy.*

—*What did they do?*

At night, they would take the old boy to the prostitute. They would call the whore aside and ask her to show him tenderness. Just affection, without addenda or pudenda. After all, the old fellow was past his sell-by date. The whore should just sing him to sleep. So they fixed everything up with her, without him being aware. And they paid her extra the following day, to corroborate the lie of his success. More vigorous than any young man! Relatives and prostitute would sing the praises of the old man's lust, playing their part in the farce. As the year passed, what happened was that the girl was won over and devoted herself exclusively to the elderly grandfather. She never went with another man again. Until one day, the prostitute turned up pregnant. No one was in any doubt: the child must be the old man's.

—*And you, Massimo, why do you remember this?*

—*I am that child.*

I decided not to say anything. His confession didn't even seem true. Why was he allowing me into his secret? But the Italian continued: there was indeed such a thing as fate. His fate had brought him there, had dumped him in that remote place and even given him a prostitute who kept secrets.

—*I've been protected by the hand of a good saint.*

But only now was he able to assess this protection. Night after night he had failed to sleep for fear of being blown to pieces like the others. Didn't I know why he had been saved? If he had remained unexplodable, it was because he had benefited from generous protection. He had survived thanks to a love affair.

—*And do you believe that, Massimo? Do you believe in these things of ours?*

The important thing wasn't the truth of the matter. What mattered was that someone had intervened on his behalf. That was the only truth that interested him.

—*And who do you think it was?*

He believed it had been Temporina. His heart told him so. I knew that the old-young girl couldn't have ordered a spell. No woman can call for a medicine-man without becoming a mother.

—*It wasn't Temporina. It was another.*

He smiled, certain it had been Temporina. He continued to pack his things. On the spur of the moment, he suddenly produced a cassette. He remembered: it was the one containing Anna's statement. He had a recording there that he had taped all alone. One afternoon, when I had gone to the administration building, the Italian had paid the prostitute a visit.

—*So you've been going around without me? Without your official translator?*

The European was embarrassed. He began to justify

himself, but I let him off the blame. Massimo still hesitated. But in the end, he switched on the recorder and we both fell silent while we listened to the voice of Anna Godwilling:

Take care, Massimo Risi, sir: the mouth is big and eyes are small. Or as we say here: a donkey eats thorns with its smooth tongue. The problem is that what's happening here is more dangerous than you think. Why is it dangerous? You'll find out like a duck. Yes, like a duck that only discovers how hard things are after it has broken its beak.

It's that in the midst of it all, there's blood, people killed who haven't had their face covered. These dead people slept out in the open, sullying the night. For you, this doesn't produce serious consequences. Here, it's not death that matters, but the dead. Do you understand? Still more people are going to die, I can assure you. Don't make that face. I hope disaster will pass you by, for you seem to me to be a good man.

I was sent here by Operation Production. Who remembers that? They crammed trucks with prostitutes, thieves mixed with honest folk and sent them as far away as possible. It all happened from one day to the next, without warning, without a chance to say farewell. When you want to clean a nation, all you produce is dirt.

In Tizangara, I was well received. The folk here kept their distance, as if they didn't want to be contaminated. But they didn't treat me badly. At first, I felt as if I was in a prison without bars, but hemmed in on all sides. I was like the prisoner who finds in his gaoler the only being with whom he can exchange human thoughts. Let me ask you: why did they teach us all this shit about us being humans? It would be better if we were animals, all instinct. So that we could rape, bite and kill. Without guilt, premeditation or pardon. That's the tragedy: only a few learned the lesson of humanity.

On one occasion, I ran away. I set off into the bush, as far as where the forest gets untangled even without any wind. I fell to the ground as if dead, next to a bridge over a dried-up river. I was aware of someone approaching and lifting me up in their arms. I was as light as a bat's entrails. I was carried to a beautiful house, my eyes had never been trained to contemplate such beauty. I never identified who had looked after me: I was exhausted, my vision was impeded by mists and dizziness. Then, once I could look after myself, I was left in the church. Nowadays, I wonder whether it was all a dream. The house never existed. And if it did, then it has fallen down, collapsed into dust without memory. The thing is that all the women in the world sleep out in the open. As if all were widows and subject to the rituals of purification. As if all the homes had fallen ill. And the whole world were in mourning. Sometimes, in brief moments of happiness, we pretend to take our rest under our lost roof. Sometimes, I fancy I hear the voice that saved me, the house that gave me shelter.

These people in power here in Tizangara fear their own pettiness. They are imprisoned in their desire to get rich. For the people won't forgive them for their failure to distribute wealth. Round here, the moral is: get rich, yes for sure, but never alone. They are harried by the poor from within and scorned by the rich from without. I feel sorry for them, poor souls, for they are forever lackeys.

And so I learned my pieces of wisdom: I pass like a shadow across the sun. I'm a very well-connected person. Like those little birds that find their food in the mouth of a crocodile. I pick the dirt from between its teeth and it welcomes me. I protect myself by making my home in the midst of danger. My life is a giving and taking of favours, I conduct my business between the teeth and jaws of murderers.

Learn this, my friend. Do you know why I liked you? It happened when I watched you crossing the road, the way you walked. You can measure a man by his gait. You were walking by yourself, all childlike and contrite, like a little boy who always attends his lessons. That's what I liked. You're a good man, I could see that straightaway. Do you remember I spoke to you on the first day you were here? There where you come from, there are also good folk. And that's enough for me to keep my hopes up. Even if it's only one good one. Just one is enough for me.

The moment I saw you on that first day, I said to myself: this one's going to survive. For round here, you need to keep your wisdom to yourself in order to get by. Do you know the difference between a wise white and a wise black? The white man's wisdom is measured by the speed with which he answers you. Among us, the wisest is the one who takes the longest to answer. Some are so wise they never answer.

You do well, Massimo: don't aspire to be the centre of attention. Self-importance here is lethal. Watch, for example, those little birds that perch on the back of hippos. Their might is their diminutive scale. That is our skill, our way of becoming greater. Feeding off the backs of the mighty.

I'm sorry, I have to interrupt this statement of mine, but you are confusing me. Why are you looking at me like that? You desire me, don't you, Massimo? But it can't be. I can't do it with you. If you touch me, you'll die.

—I can protect myself, I've got a contraceptive.

—It's not that. It's another type of illness.

—So how will I die?

—The women here have been given treatment ...

—What treatment?

—Don't ask questions, Massimo. Let it be, someone will explain everything to you later.

Who knows, later maybe we'll meet far away from all this? For now, I'm just going to tell you what happened that night with the Zambian. I've never told anyone, you're the first to know what happened. Well, this soldier paid me a visit and showed no manners at all. The man didn't waste his time with kisses. You know what my folk are like. He mounted me without any ado, with more slobber than a puppy. And so he used me there and then, on top of me, stark naked except for the beret on his head. He was sweating, leaking water through every pore, groaning, full of gasps. His sighs and moans got louder and more frequent, and I was just relieved the thing was nearly over and done with. Then it happened: instead of coming, the fellow burst, with a huge bang. I almost died of fright. I shut my eyes. I'd heard about this, foreigners exploding when they mounted girls. But it had never happened to me, never. I didn't even want to open my eyes, to see all the blood splashed about, and his insides hanging from the lampshade. But in the end, I didn't have to clean anything. The man had exploded like a balloon. The creature had burst into smithereens without leaving a trace.

Now go. Turn round and don't come back. Don't even peep at me. For you would see me looking at you with desire. Go, and visit me some other time.

18   The manuscript voice of Sulplício

What I wanted was to die, a victim
of the best of life's recipes:
a good drink and bad women.
(Sulplício's statement)

That morning, my father arrived when Massimo was still asleep. The old man invited himself into my room and peered at everything just as a dog sniffs at his doubts. He paused by the table where the Italian had left his tape recorder.

—*Is this the machine that photographs voices?*

—*Yes.*

—*You should be ashamed, my son. Ashamed.*

—*Ashamed of what?*— I asked.

For him, it was obvious: how could I go around capturing the words of my fellow countrymen in a box like that? Once inside that box, what would the fate of our voices be? Who could be sure it wasn't for casting spells over there in Europe? Spells directed against our wretched land, which had already suffered so much.

I decided to give him an explanation. My old man was isolated from life's modernities. Tizangara was very far, and he was very remote. But to my surprise, even before I began my explanation, my father asked me to switch the recorder on.

—*Put that wretched machine on.*

—*Why, father?*

—*I want to see my voice written on it.*

And Sulplício spoke. I asked him to get nearer to the microphone. He said he wasn't going to betray any confidences to the machine. That his voice was strong. And then he addressed me with some unforgettable words. What he said was recorded. He overcame his fear of being taken advantage of for malicious purposes. Here are his words:

For you, my son, for you who studied in school, the ground is a sheet of paper, everything is written on it. For us, the earth is a mouth, the soul of a seashell. Time is the snail that shapes this shell. We put our ear to the shell and we hear the beginning of it all, when everything was of yore.

My first memory is the men hunting flamingos. We lived on the shore of those lakes, right there where the great birds graze. Your grandfather used to take me and your uncle out hunting. He was teaching us to be men, with their burden of cruelty. Your uncle hid behind a tree in the mangrove. He held a long stick in his hand. My father walked away, growing tiny in the distance beyond the salt pits. I watched him fade into the mist beyond that pinkish stain, while the noon haze turned everything into a mirage.

Suddenly, your grandfather was running and clapping his hands, shouting to scare the creatures away. Was the flamingo invented after the aeroplane? What's for sure is that they don't fly straight up into the air like the other birds. They accelerate gradually in order to take to the air. And those flamingos would unfurl their necks, raise their feet, ruffle the marshes with their long legs. The watery ground seemed to reject speed, hindering the arrival of death.

And there they went, those lanky creatures, undignified in their escape. And there was your uncle getting ready, hidden by the trunk of the tree. Suddenly, the stick was slashing the air, thwack! And it was a stick hitting a stick, you could hear the crack, the bird's legs suddenly revealing new knees and collapsing to the ground like a skinny tree when struck by lightning.

Once knocked down, the bird looked like a pink ribbon twisting on a sheet of ash. In its death throes, its white plumage turned grey, its neck turned into a blind snake.

Your uncle jumped out from the tree shouting. I stood rooted to the ground, watching the sad scene. My father ran up and ordered:

—Kufa mbalame!

It was the order to kill the bird. In my brother's hands, the stick completed its task and the creature breathed its last. That blow settled in my soul. The bird was dying inside me. Worse, however, was still to come. At night, I was obliged to eat the meat. My father thought I wasn't hard enough, not ready enough to kill. So I had to eat its remains. In order to be a man. I refused.

—Eat it, young fellow. Pretend it's fish.

And he beat me. Until, when it was already dark, I pretended to chew that flesh. On one such night, I cursed my old man. And do you know what? He died that very same night. I even heard his screams, he was trembling all over, and a green foam seeped out of his mouth. Your uncle blamed me, and turned all his rage on me. From then on, he persecuted me, damaging my pride:

—That one there is a bit of a sissy.

I felt weak, haunted by shame. Killing flamingos was a test of male power that I had failed. So I became dispirited, downtrodden, humiliated. Until I got to know your mother and she saved me from that bottomless pit. Men are like that, pretending they're strong because they're afraid. She touched me lightly and said:

—You're strong. You don't need to prove anything to anyone.

Then, she invented the story of the flamingo. She said it was a legend, a tale of origins. But it was a lie. She herself had invented it, just so as to lay my ghosts to rest.

My father fell silent. He was all emotional, and his throat was tight with longing. He went outside and stayed on the veranda, watching the night. From where he was, he spoke to me:

—*Now turn it back and start playing it. I want to listen to myself.*

I let the recorder reproduce his words, so recently uttered that they seemed like an echo. He listened to himself in awe, nodding his head in constant agreement. In the end, he re-emphasised his order with another one:

—*And I don't want that Italian listening to my words. Do you hear? I don't trust that son-of-a-bitch one hundred per cent yet.*

—*But father, that Italian is helping us.*

—*Helping?*

—*He and the others. They're helping us build peace.*

—*That's where you're mistaken. It's not peace they're interested in. What they're concerned with is order, the regime of this world.*

—*Now, father ...*

—*Their problem is to keep the order that enables them to be boss. That type of order has been our history's sickness.*

According to him, the division of existences had been reborn within us as a result of that sickness: some were lackeys of the bosses and others lackeys of the lackeys. The powerful – those from outside and those within – had only one aim: to show that the only way we could be governed was if we were colonised.

—*You said a little while ago that I wasn't modern.*

—*It wasn't meant badly, father. I was referring to the recorder ...*

—*Once upon a time we wanted to be civilised. Now we want to be modern.*

When all was said and done, we continued to be prisoners of the desire not to be ourselves. Old Sulplício, at that moment, seemed too verbose. He feared he might be squandering his thoughts. And then, after a pause, he added:

—*Wipe my voice off, I don't want any funny business.*

19   The revelations

It's the darkness that dresses the hippopotamus.
(Proverb)

Very early next morning, the Italian went out with Temporina. She was going down to the river to say goodbye to Father Muhando. I decided to go to the administrator's residence to inform him that the UN delegate was getting ready to leave. However, no sooner had I got to the entrance than I came upon a scene of utter confusion. There was shouting and the noise of people scuffling. The door was ajar, and I went in without waiting to be invited. In the reception room were Estêvão Jonas, Chupanga and Anna Godwilling. None of them saw me come in.

Estêvão Jonas was holding Anna Godwilling by the arm. He was pulling her towards him and then pushing her up against the wall. And he was screaming: whore, you whore, you whore! That she was being put under arrest, charged with the deaths of the foreigners. Chupanga was asking for calm. By this time, the prostitute was on the floor and the administrator's foot flew in her direction. Anna Godwilling, propping herself up on one arm, raised her head and screamed:

—*You're a shit! I'm going to denounce you!*

Another kick. Anna was bleeding, her face was losing its contours. I made myself visible, to see if I could stop the violence. The administrator looked at me. Astonished. For sure, he was going to order me to leave. But Anna Godwilling's voice could be heard above the racket:

—*You're the one killing people. It's you, Estêvão Jonas!*

—*Shut up!*

—*You're the one who orders mines to be laid! You're the one who kills our brothers.*

—*Don't listen, she's crazy*— he said to me.

—*I saw you laying mines, I saw ...*

Estêvão was at the end of his tether. He ordered Chupanga:

—*Get rid of this female!*

—*You, Jonas, don't touch that woman!*

The order came from the doorway. We all turned and came face to face with Ermelinda, her arms akimbo. Estêvão even rubbed his eyes when he saw her. This time, his wife really did have the bearing of a lady, the very first lady. And once again, she gave the order:

—*Don't touch that woman!*

—*You keep out of this, Ermelinda. And you, Chupanga, didn't you hear my command? Get rid of this parcel.*

—*Don't move, Chupanga*— countermanded Ermelinda.

Chupanga, strangely enough, didn't move. Was he disobeying his boss for the very first time? Estêvão watched all this, flabbergasted. The First Lady crossed the room and knelt down next to Anna Godwilling. Passing her hand over her head, she said:

—*You're going to be all right, sister!*

Anna's eyes were two windows of astonishment. As if at last she remembered the voice she sought from the past, the mist-shrouded soul who had blessed her with life again. It had, indeed, been none other than Ermelinda who had taken her in and given her a first place of refuge in Tizangara.

The prostitute timidly drew in her neck to receive the other woman's caress, and they both wept. We men listened in silence. They were the exclusive mistresses of what was happening there. As they walked across the room, Ermelinda could be heard saying:

—*Get out of this house, Estêvão.*

—*Get out of my house!? And where shall I go?*

—*Go and stay with Jonassane. I never want to see you again.*

And the two women went out. Chupanga called the administrator aside and they stood talking in undertones for several minutes. They were certainly discussing Ermelinda's unexpected transformation. I took a guess at their explanation for this: the woman was following the advice of Zeca Andorinho. Yes, that was it, because for them, when a woman has an idea, it comes from another man's head. All of a sudden, the adjutant got up and took his leave. He turned to me and invited me to leave with him.

Chupanga was in a hurry. He ordered me to return to the guesthouse, to be with the foreigner. He jumped into his car and accelerated away in a cloud of dust. I walked along the paths down to the river. I found Massimo with Father Muhando. Temporina was sitting next to the tree. I told them what had happened. Temporina immediately took a decision: she went off in the direction of the administrator's residence. She was going to lend her support to Anna Godwilling, join the other women. All of them together made up another race.

We said nothing, while Father Muhando waved his arm as if he were punching the air.

—*I had my suspicions all along!*

He'd already discovered the plot, but the powers that be in the place had prepared a trap for him. The plan was simple and sufficient for its purpose – one or two drinks were enough. When it came to it, the man of the cloth drank his tipple not only out of love, but devotion. They took advantage of the priest's vice and excavated it to its limits. To the point where the priest had become converted to unbelief.

—*Do you understand now, my dear foreigner?*

In the words of the priest, the twin coincidences were as clear as they were improbable. What was happening was as follows: a proportion of the landmines that were found, were then returned to the same patch of ground. In Tizangara, everything was mixed: the war of business and the business of war. When the war ended, there were landmines left over, yes of course. Some. But not enough to prolong the mine clearance programmes. The money siphoned off from these programmes was a source of revenue that the local leaders couldn't do without. It was the administrator's stepson who hatched the plan: what if they fiddled the numbers, invented endless threats? It was worth it. Landmines were planted and unplanted. A few deaths here and there were even convenient, to give the plan more credibility. But they were nameless people, in the interior of an African country that could hardly sustain its name in the world. Who would worry about that?

—*But then came this troublesome incident!*

—*What incident, Father?*

The death of the blue helmets. When foreigners began to get blown up, the scam fell apart. The bangs grew louder and threatened the fraud. They attracted inappropriate attention. The truth about the landmines required evidence of blood. But the blood of the nation. No cross-border haemorrhages. Faced with the possibility that the scandal might burst, the administrator summoned the witchdoctor and gave the order for it to stop forthwith. No more UN soldiers should disappear.

—*And what was Zeca Andorinho's answer?*

Zeca lied, said that it was a spell that had been cast from outside. That these were extra-local phenomena, commanded by forces beyond their control. And he said he had no hand in such supernatural events.

—*So what do we do now, Father Muhando?*

—*Aren't you from the United Nations? You should save us, Senhor Massimo.*

Massimo didn't react to the irony. His head was all of a muddle: his decision to leave, to abandon Tizangara, seemed to have been thrown into doubt. But he was incapable of thinking. It was Muhando who offered an opinion:

—*It would be a good idea to go and catch that rogue of an administrator. Him and his servant boy, Chupanga.*

Suddenly, Temporina appeared, running. She was in a state of agitation, almost deranged. She stumbled through the news she brought. Chupanga had gone back to the administration building to fetch Estêvão Jonas. At that very moment, the administrator was travelling by car to join his stepson in the neighbouring country. When he returned, Chupanga would pass by the dam to carry out his orders.

—*What orders?*

—*They've given the order for the dam to be blown up.*

—*Blow up the dam? What for?*

—*So that all this land will be flooded. That way, the evidence of their crimes, this whole story of mines being laid, will be wiped out.*

We looked at each other in astonishment. If the dam exploded, the fields would be swallowed up by the water. The situation was developing to such an extent that it seemed unreal. To add to the confusion, my father appeared from the direction of the river. He was with Zeca Andorinho and other old men. I told him the news and he gave his instructions immediately:

—*Go, son, hurry to avoid this tragedy. Go to the dam before that devil gets there.*

We got ready to go straightaway. The frontier was right there, beyond the river. Chupanga wouldn't take long. Some of the old folk joined me. Massimo Risi was also getting his things ready. My father declared:

—*You go, son. But don't take that white man with you.*

—*I want to go*— the Italian said decisively.

—*You're not going. Son: I'm giving you an order. That white stays!*

—*Why, father?*

—*Because this is a matter we've got to settle ourselves. We alone know how to handle this. Don't you see?*

Father Muhando put his arm round the foreigner's shoulder. Was he comforting him for being excluded? Zeca Andorinho shook his head, as if laying the matter to rest, and added:

—*We've had enough of asking others to resolve our problems.*

I got ready to leave. The witchdoctor would go with me along with the others who had gathered there. We organised ourselves in groups. Some would go up the river to warn people along the banks to move away. Others would go by road, trying to get there before the order could be carried out, and thus avoid a disaster. My old man called me and said:

—*Take this pistol and kill that Chupanga for me!*

I didn't have ears for such words. Kill? Yes, kill that worm, who wasn't even human. I refused, without blood and without voice.

—*Don't worry yourself, because the creature's not a man. He's just an animal.*

—*But father, don't you remember? You couldn't even bring yourself to kill the flamingo when you were told to.*

—*I've already told you, blow that devil's brains out. Even Father Muhando here will bless you. Isn't that so, Father?*

Zeca Andorinho took possession of it: he snatched the pistol from my hand and stuffed it in his belt. And he said:

—*I'll see that justice is done myself*— and pointing to the revolver, he added: —*This will be my first piece of magic!*

The first group set off. I stayed behind, riven by a thousand doubts. My steps were darkened by shame. My old man's hand on my shoulder brought me to my senses. What he told me, I'll never forget.

—*Just as well you didn't accept my order to kill. I'm happy.*

—*Really?*

—*Now, I'm even more your father than before.*

Not that we do this sort of thing where we come from, but I gave old Sulplício a lingering hug. I didn't even know whether it was because I was leaving or had just arrived. He pushed me away. He didn't want to reveal his weakness in front of the others.

—*Now, remember my words. Don't forget the little path, the one that passes by the termite nest. If the world ...*

—*The world isn't going to end, father.*

—*Mine already has, son.*

Massimo asked us not to leave immediately. He wanted to talk to Zeca Andorinho. He asked for no more than a quick, brief moment. He spoke openly and out loud:

—*Please release Temporina from her spell!*

He wanted Andorinho to give his beloved back her age. None of us spoke. The foreigner didn't know it, but these were not matters to be brought up in the light of day. And he was insistent, afraid of not being understood:

—*Give her back her youth.*

We were sure the witchdoctor would be angry and put out. But Zeca Andorinho smiled and answered him:

—*You've already given it back to her.*

And he had the following suggestion to make: the foreigner should go and find her to say goodbye. For he shouldn't even think of taking Temporina away with him. The land keeps people's roots. But a woman is the root of the land.

—*But look, see who's coming!*

It seemed a coincidence: there on the first strip of horizon, they saw Temporina coming towards them, walking happily, almost a mirage. The Italian didn't waste any time. He shot off down a path, alone, running like a rabbit. Until there was a sudden echoing yell:

—*Stop, Massimo, the track is mined!*

Massimo didn't understand immediately. By the time he stopped, he was already some way down the perilous path. There was nothing but a stony silence. Everything at a standstill. We on one side, Temporina on the other. There, hidden in the ground lay something that would make him lie down. The foreigner stood frozen in the middle of the landscape, his legs trembling before the ground's fatality. No one knew what to do. He had already penetrated deep into the terrain. It would be as dangerous to go back as it would be to go forward. As for rescuing him – how could anyone do that? Suddenly, Temporina unleashed a strange command:

—*Come on, Massimo. Come to me!*

Was this love in all its madness? How could she invite him to risk the path? Father Muhando issued a countermand:

—*Don't move!*

From this side, other voices joined in chorus. The Italian should stay where he was. But Temporina insisted, gently summoning him:

—*Don't you remember how I taught you to tread the ground? Well, come, and walk the way I taught you how.*

Massimo hesitated. But then – could it be faith? – he started to walk. Slowly, his whole body was a heel, one foot in front of the other, he stepped without leaving a footprint. And before our astonished gaze, Massimo Risi passed across the mined terrain, just as Jesus had walked on the waters.

20 The ancestors' estranged children

Ash flies, but it's fire that has wings.
(A saying from Tizangara)

We had left the town that night. Risi stayed behind in
Temporina's arms, in his room at the guesthouse. The men
of the town advanced against the current of time, up the
river. They were trying to avoid a tragedy. One group had
left in dugouts. I was following on foot, among mosquitoes
and darkness. In the end, we didn't get far. For those who
were travelling by road caught Chupanga. They brought
him to Tizangara, to face Zeca Andorinho and my father.
We all crowded around under the great fig tree. He wasn't
the one responsible for carrying out the plan. His version
was full of repentance: that he'd returned of his own free
will to denounce everything. That he would never obey the
orders that Estêvão had given. That he had wanted to
distance himself from power for a long time. With the
arrival of the Italian, he had thought the moment right to
blow the whistle on the whole thing.

—*Didn't I try to talk to the Italian?*

He wanted me to confirm this. But I kept myself to myself and said nothing. Chupanga's exhibition of himself made me cringe.

—*If you refused to obey, why were you going in the direction of the dam?*

Precisely to make sure that no one else got there. That was the alibi. My father got up and said in a loud voice:

—*Kill this fellow for me, Zeca.*

—*No. The Italian will know you killed me.*

—*And so what?*

—*You've got to respect human rights.*

Laughter all around. Chupanga began to cry. He asked for mercy. After all, he hadn't carried out what Estêvão had ordered him to do. And what was more, he was planning to create a political opposition. Yes, the country, the future, the international world: everything demanded greater democracy. And he had been born for politics, it was his vocation, ever since the cradle. The new political force was already at the planning stage. Turning to my old man, Chupanga said:

—*I'd even thought of offering you responsibility for the Tizangara district. You've got the respect of the masses.*

For one moment, I expected to hear my father's booming voice. That was really beyond his capacity for listening. But to my surprise, he replied in a mild tone:

—*You don't understand. I would only accept a higher post.*

—*At provincial level?*

—*Higher.*

—*National?*

—Higher, still higher.

The others thought this was megalomania. But only I knew that my father was referring to other dimensions, another height. That intangible level, where neither men nor their infelicities stand out.

Zeca made a sign to my father. I understood: it was a case of impure evil. They forgave him for his wretched life. But the following day, he was to take the First Lady away. And take her to Estêvão. Chupanga replied that Estêvão didn't want to take possession of his wife again. If only because he had a woman on the other side of the frontier, whom he had been keeping for a long time.

—It's precisely because of that. We're delivering his punishment to him.

And they all dispersed. I was left alone with my father. We settled down on the veranda of our old house. It was night. We shared a few chunks of bread, drank some tea.

—Don't tell the Italian about any of this.

I asked him if he now viewed the foreigner in a better light. Sulplício remained silent. He swatted one of those insects that are attracted by lights. The creature was stunned.

—Is it dead?

—It's just pretending.

Then he compared himself to it. There are those who make themselves dead in time of difficulty. He was pretending to be alive. For almost all of him had been carried away by one death. Only a tiny part of him remained on this side. It wasn't the foreigner he cared about. It was us, our dispersed family.

—*You know, these days spent with you have made me yearn to live again.*

A man without a woman, without a child, is like someone without a mirror. He had become slovenly, unshaven and dirty because we were far away. He had no one to care about him. Nor did he have anyone to care about.

—*Now, I want you nearby, son. Is that too much to wish for?*

The lump in my throat prevented me from answering. He realised how vulnerable I was, and went on quickly so that my emotions shouldn't be noticed. I was, after all, a man.

—*It's just that in my neglect, I am reminded of the state of our own land.*

For our country didn't receive the care of its native sons. Had I ever noticed where our land was being taken? It was like the man who had been brought back to life so often that he ended up dying. I should see how our land had been riddled with holes. Some laid mines. They were the ones from outside. Others, those within, were placing the country inside a mine.

—*You know what's worse, son?*

—*What's that, father?*

—*It's that our ancestors now look at us, their children, like strangers.*

My old man was getting into issues that were too complex for my understanding. He couldn't see that I was sometimes incapable of grasping the meaning of his words.

—*You know what your mother used to say? The best place for a cry was the veranda.*

And it made sense: the veranda. Before it lay the world and all its infinities; behind, lay the house, the first source of refuge. With one extravagant gesture, my old man brought our conversation to an end. At the front door, he declared:

—*You can tell that foreign friend of yours that tomorrow I'll show him what happened to the exploded soldiers.*

—*Really, father?*

He nodded and disappeared into his room. I was happy for Risi. He would, after all, be able to bring his mission to a conclusion. I drifted into sleep. What I dreamed hurt me. So much so that I awoke with a heavy feeling in my heart. Fragments of dream mingled with memories. Everything in little bits, all mixed up. I hadn't exploded but my dream had burst. This was what remained from that night, between memory and delirium: in the dream, I was sitting on top of the termite hill, the last place in the world. All around me was water, the overflow of all the rivers. The hill was the only island in sight. Here and there, the surface was broken by the crowns of trees. These pinnacles were the only places where birds could rest.

Sitting there stranded on top of the anthill, I recalled my personal life. My life's end was, after all, a return to my primal beginning. For there where I was coming to my end, the last place on earth, had been the first place in my life. I was closing a cycle. It had been on just such a hill that my mother had buried the placenta that, for nine months, had been my wrapping. That first blanket of mine had been given its burial on the western side of a hill like this one. It's taken as a truth in Tizangara: the ants' nest is the navel of the soil. And we always lived next to a huge anthill. There, behind the path that my father had suggested I take to flee the end of the world, there it stood in defiance of time. The anthill had been the centre of my existence. Whenever a storm threatened, my uncle would busy himself taking earth from the hill.

—*There in church, the priest distributes holy water. Here we have holy earth. This here!*— he would say as he let the sand run through his fingers.

And he would sprinkle the sand over the house. I would ask why he was doing this. But he avoided elaborate explanations. I was a child, a being who was barred from the understanding of sacred subjects. And that earth was an intimate matter. It was my mother who explained it to me:

—*This soil from the hill is to stop the wind blowing our house away.*

The sand from the hill was an earthen anchor dropped in our land. Our house was a boat moored to our lives. There would be neither river nor wind. My mother had fulfilled her role as a woman. I had not fulfilled mine as a son. Hence her blindness in me. If it hadn't been for life, I would surely have been more touchable.

Now, tens of years later, there I was, a solitary survivor, sitting on the last residue of the world. The force of the current passing by carried with it ox horns, trunks of pod mahogany, the roofs of straw huts. The remains of everything, as if the whole land had been shipwrecked. As if the River Madzimadzi were in flood.

That was when I saw it approaching like a raft. It was being swept along by the current of the river. It was, in fact, an island without root. On top of it, waving his arms, I saw the simpleton. It was he who was at the island's helm. That barge-like craft passed by the anthill without stopping. I shouted and seemed to be able to make myself heard, but no one could see me. And there, at the edge of the island, I could see my mother, along with Aunt Hortensia. The other dead people seemed to be peering through the mists as if they were looking for something. I jumped up and down and yelled in despair. But they couldn't see me. My father's words came to me in all their weight: our ancestors look at us as if we were strangers. And when they see us, they no longer recognise us.

Last chapter: A land swallowed up by the earth

What I remember I never speak about.
I only yearn for what I never recall.
What's the use of memory
if what I lived most intensely
is what never happened?
(Sulplício's talk)

Massimo Risi returned home only at the end of the
following day, when it was getting dark. His time spent
with Temporina had put stars in his eyes. They were stars,
indeed, but in a sky of sadness.

That night, my father vanished into the darkness after
his meal. He was walking towards the river, among the
tallest grass. For the first time, I followed, watching closely
to see if there was any truth in his fantasy about hanging
up his skeleton. It was then that behind some bushes, I was
surprised by a sight that sent a shiver through my soul: my
father was taking the bones from his body and hanging

them on the branches of a tree. With great care and method, he hung his bits of bone, one by one, on that improvised clothes-hanger.

Afterwards, devoid of his inner frame, he grew flaccid, dissolving on to the ground. There he remained, spread out and lifeless, like some sighing mass, or a shapeless sponge. His jaws were the only bones he kept. For talking, as he explained later. In case he had to shout, to summon help urgently.

My father noticed my presence and gave me a furious look. Then, pointing to his suspended skeleton, he said in a panic:

—*Don't let that white man find us here. I don't want him to see me like this. Go and find out where the fellow has got to.*

The foreigner was asleep, in the embrace of our old house. I sighed as I looked up into the night. What were we doing there, in the middle of the bush, next to a bend in the River Madzimadzi? From where we were, we could see the tamarind tree, back there in the garden of our house, and I shivered: from the top of the highest branch, an owl was peering at us. To be precise, it had its eye on my old man.

Now lying there, almost devoid of weight, my father looked as fragile as a snail without a shell. He seemed to guess my thoughts. He asked me to push him over to the matumi tree. He wanted to be next to his hanging bonework. These were precautions in response to a fright he'd got the previous night: at the dead of night he heard noises. He was startled. And what if a hyena were gnawing his bones? His body was sore where he had parts missing. And it was. Or rather they were. Not hyenas as such. But false hyenas, mulattos of creatures and people. And not only this: their heads were those of the town's leaders. Here was a parade of political leaders in an animal's body. Each one was carrying in its mouth so many ribs, spines and jawbones. My father tried to raise himself and get away as far as possible. But like that, filleted and without his inner frame, all he could do was slide around like a worm, twisting and turning like an invertebrate. When he saw these powerful folk snuffling around among bones, he asked himself: how do they get so fat if there is no longer anyone alive for them to hunt, if all that's left is destitution? One of the hyenas answered him like this:

—*Well, we steal and steal again. We steal from the state, we steal from the country until only the bones are left.*

—*Then we gnaw everything, we regurgitate it all and we eat again*— said another hyena.

What they would do with me was to sell my flesh to the foreign lions outside. They, the local hyenas, would satisfy themselves with the skeleton. Suddenly, the storm burst and the monsters disappeared. The multiple bones from so many different bodies lay scattered on the ground. My father dragged himself painfully around among this skeletal collection. How could he tell his own bones from the rest? Bones are more like each other than are stones.

—*I knew they wanted to steal our souls. But bones …* Sulplício paused in his recollection of the dream, and said in a different tone: —*Now you've come and found me in this state.*

—*I'm sorry, father. I never believed that you did this. I always had my doubts.*

—*I've done many things you don't know about.*

How he dreamed better without the weight of his bones! His de-boned body, he was wont to say, was like a cloud on the loose.

—*You should do the same, it's easy to learn how. Like this, a person can even dream himself.*

—*But father, leaving our intimacies up in a tree?*

—*Can you think of a more sacred perch? And I'll tell you this: go and choose your tree carefully, for it will be your most immortal companion.*

I smiled with him, but with an oblique sadness: my old man and I had spent such little time together in lighthearted fun. That was when I heard Massimo Risi's footsteps. The foreigner had woken up and left home to look for us. My father reacted hurriedly:

—*Quickly, cover me with that blanket!*

I threw the cover over him, concealing his unshaped body. The foreigner sat down and patted his uniform. There's dust that isn't loosened with the pat of a hand. On the contrary, the dirt is spread around. The Italian, thus covered in dust, looked as if he were being eaten by the earth. The man contemplated the darkness. Never had the night seemed so immense. Then he asked:

—*Well then, Senhor Sulplício: are you going to explain why my men disappeared, or not?*

—*It's not I who am going to talk. It's this place that will do the talking.*

—*This place?*

—*Yes, this very place. That's why we came here. Otherwise, I would have talked back there in town.*

My father explained: he would only talk in the place that was sacred to him, next to the River Madzimadzi. The three of us were on the riverbank, watching the flow of the river. And old Sulplício declared:

—*I follow Father Muhando: I too talk with God here.*

The Italian listened as if he understood nothing. He shook his head and made to get up and go. For a moment, he gave my father a puzzled look. His frown almost made me fear that he had guessed my father's boneless state. But the foreigner returned to the big house and, for some time, the light of his candle continued to glimmer through the curtain.

We too, my father and I, lay down. We huddled together in the open air, enveloped in the night. In the batting of an eyelid, he fell asleep. I even heard the Italian approaching. Inside the house, the heat was unbearable and he preferred to put up with the mosquitoes. He was carrying a bag and blanket. He laid everything out on the ground. The bag with his things inside it served as a pillow. It wasn't long before he was asleep. Then, I too fell into a slumber.

It happened all of a sudden: I woke up with a start. On my face I felt the burning blast of an inferno. I looked to one side and almost fainted: there where the earth had been, there was nothing but a huge abyss. There was no landscape left, not even any ground. We were on the edge of a bottomless chasm. I warned my father, and he was immediately agitated:

—*My bones?*

Of the tree there was neither sign nor shade. The bones had fallen into the hole. Like the entire landscape, the house, the town, the road, everything swallowed by the void. What had happened? A man digs a big hole, fine. Many men dig a huge hole. But a cavern of that dimension was the work of the supernatural.

We called the Italian, who couldn't believe his eyes: had the entire country disappeared? Yes, the nation had been completely swallowed up in that emptiness. Facing the very last edge of the world, before the deepest crack he had ever seen, Massimo Risi gaped.

—*My reports!!? Where are my files?*

We didn't understand his great fears. But he explained, almost sobbing: the briefcase with his reports was in the town, in the room at the administration building. It had vanished like everything else into the vortex, the nothingness. How would he explain this to his superiors? How could he report that a whole country had disappeared? He would be demoted. Worse: committed for being dangerously insane.

The Italian approached the edge of the precipice. He felt giddy and stepped back, his hands clasping the back of his neck. He seemed to be on the point of fainting. My old man spoke:

—*Carry me away from the edge. We're not safe here.*

Massimo and I busied ourselves with lifting him. My father weighed less than an empty sack. What was more, he was devoid of any shape, so gelatinous that his looseness seeped out between our arms.

—*I'm hard to carry, aren't I? That's so you should realise that bones may be heavy, but they make us light.*

We moved away from the huge hole. We sat down in the shade of the forest. Then, my father summoned us. His face was solemn, his voice grave: he knew why the nation had disappeared in that bottomless crater.

—*This is the work of the ancestors ...*

—*No. The ancestors yet again!?*

—*Have some respect, Senhor Massimo. This is our business.*

My old man went on: he'd already been forewarned. Folk were made aware of what the spirits were thinking and even Zeca Andorinho had told him exactly the same thing – the ancestors weren't happy with the way things were going in the country. Such was the sad judgement of the dead upon the state of the living.

The same thing had happened in other lands in Africa. The fate of nations had been entrusted to the ambitious, who governed like hyenas, only thinking about getting fat fast. Against these failures in governance, the unthinkable had been tried: little magic bones, goat's blood, fortune-telling, incense. Stones had been kissed, saints prayed to. All had been to no avail: there had been no improvements in these countries. People were needed who loved the land. Men were needed to make other men show some respect.

Seeing that there was no solution, the gods decided to transport those countries to the skies that can be found in the depths of the earth. And they took them down to an area of subterranean fog, down there where the clouds are born. In that place, where nothing had ever made any shade, each country would remain suspended, awaiting a favourable time when they would be able to return to their own ground. At that point, those territories could be nations, with a yearned-for flag stuck in them. Until then, they would be nothing but empty nothingness, a hiccup in time. Until then, people, animals, plants, rivers and mountains would remain swallowed up by the depths. They would not be converted into spirits or ghosts, for those are creatures that emerge after death. And these hadn't died. They were transmuted into non-beings, shadows awaiting their respective people.

—*Do you understand, Senhor Massimo?*

—*More or less ...*

—*Well, you don't seem too sure.*

The Italian didn't offer anything else by way of reply. He got up, defeated. He was approaching the end of his career, the collapse of his very powers of reason. This wasn't the moment for my father to tell him fairy tales. He spoke as if deep within him:

—*This is worse than the devil's work.*

—*You mentioned the devil. And you're right. Let me explain ...*

—*I can do without any more explanations.*

The devil explained things, yes. It could well be that the hole was the work of the gods, who wanted to bury the devils who were growing fat here in our land. But there were so many that they had to dig deep, deeper than the world itself.

The Italian was no longer listening. He sat down, his head between his knees. From time to time, he would plead in a low voice:

—*My report. What am I going to write, how am I going to explain?*

—*Stop worrying, my friend. Look at me: how I miss my*

bones. They've gone. I'll never have any stiffness again. And yet I'm not crying.

For some time, we surrendered to a despair of the soul, our eyes fixed on the precipice. That was when we saw a dugout coming towards us over the abyss. It floated across the silence, suspended in the mist. It was flying through the air. Sulplício asked in a barely audible whisper, as if his voice too had lost its backbone:

—*Who is it?*

There was no answer. No one in the dugout. The little craft emerged from the mist and came to rest by the edge of the precipice. Only I got up to peer into the boat. And there lay the unexpected present.

—*Father, your bones are here!*

In his doubt, he didn't even turn his face. Without looking at me, he asked me to show him one of the bones, any one. I chose one of the bigger ones and brought it to him. He peeped at the piece of skeleton without touching it.

—*Yes, they're my bones.*

With our help, he got dressed round his bones once again. He tried some movements, tested his joints and cartilage. He felt young, rejuvenated. And he even joked:

—*This is the truth: a cow without a tail can't swat flies.*

What orders was my father obeying as he climbed into the dugout? The boat rocked as if afloat. Sulplício held out his arms to the white man and said:

—*Come!*

The white refused, his eyes aghast. My father insisted: didn't he want to come and hear the truth about what had happened?

—*Come and I'll show you where the exploded soldiers are.*

The foreigner refused and refused again to embark. I waited, my heart in suspense, for my old man to invite me aboard.

—*You stay, son.*

—*But father …*

—*Stay, I've already told you. So that you can tell others what happened to our world. I don't want the outsider here recounting this story of ours.*

And the dugout set off, hovering over nothing. When it was already far away, it seemed to me less like a boat, more like a bird. A flamingo flying off into the beyond. Until all was mist, all clouded.

Only silence was left. Then the Italian went to the bag, which he had turned into a pillow, and took out a pen and a piece of paper, and methodically scribbled some tidy sentences. I looked over his sad shoulder and read what he was writing. There was the fat title: 'Last Report'. And the rest read as follows:

His Excellency
The Secretary-General of the United Nations

It is my painful duty to have to report the complete disappearance of a country in strange and almost inexplicable circumstances. I am aware that the present report will lead to my dismissal from the team of United Nations advisers. However, I have no other choice but to report the truth that confronts me: that this vast country has disappeared, as if by a stroke of magic. There is no land left, no people, and even the very ground has evaporated into an immense chasm. I write from the edge of this world, next to the last survivor of this nation.

The Italian paused, his trembling pen pointing towards the precipice that opened at his feet. And he asked me:

—*Take another look over.*

—*I've already looked a thousand times.*

—*And can't you see anything?*

—*Nothing.*

—*Have you looked right down to the bottom?*

—*The problem is that there is no bottom. You'd better see for yourself.*

—*I can't. I suffer from vertigo.*

The Italian ended up sitting on the edge of the abyss. Nearby, swallows passed by, streaking across the sky, without venturing into that subterranean sky, which was more recent than the day itself.

—*What are we going to do?*— I asked.

—*Let's wait.*

His voice was calm, as if it came from some ancient wisdom.

—*Wait for whom?*

—*Wait for another boat*— and after another pause, he corrected himself: —*wait for another flight of the flamingo. There's bound to be another one.*

He pulled out the sheet of paper on which he had just written the report for the United Nations. What was he doing? He was folding it and pressing along the folds. He was making a paper bird. He finished it with elaborate care, and then got up and launched it over the abyss. The paper bird fluttered and glided in the air, hovering almost liquidly over the absence of ground. Gradually, it descended, as if fearing the profundity of its destination.

Massimo smiled as he performed this ritual of childhood. I sat down next to him. For the first time, I felt as if the Italian was a brother, born of the same land. He looked at me and seemed to read my inner thoughts, guessing my fears.

—*There's bound to be another one*— he repeated.

I took his word as if from an elder. As I looked into the mist while we waited, I wondered whether the journey my father had embarked upon might not have been the last flight of the flamingo. Even so, I continued to sit there quietly. Waiting for another time. Until I heard my mother's song, the one she sang so that the flamingos would push the sun from the other side of the world.